Long Valley Showdown

Fallon and Ralph reined up before One Eyed Jack's saloon doors. Inside were four men who had tried to rape Fallon's Shoshone Indian wife. Neither Fallon nor Ralph knew the gunfighter with the four.

Through the red haze of his fury, Fallon could think of nothing except beating senseless the men who had assaulted his wife. But big and imposing as he was, he was no match for four men who wouldn't fight fair.

Nevertheless, without knowing what to expect, they stepped through the doors of the saloon. . . .

Long Valley Showdown

Billy Hall

A Black Horse Western

ROBERT HALE · LONDON

© Billy Hall 2006
First published in Great Britain 2006

ISBN-10: 0-7090-7891-9
ISBN-13: 978-0-7090-7891-3

Robert Hale Limited
Clerkenwell House
Clerkenwell Green
London EC1R 0HT

Typeset by Derek Doyle & Associates, Shaw Heath.
Printed and bound in Great Britain by
Antony Rowe Limited, Wiltshire.

CHAPTER 1

'Them wear war paint.'

Almost absent-mindedly he corrected her English. His eyes never flickered as he did so. They continued to stare hard into the distance.

'They are wearing war paint.'

No trace of irritation crossed her face. She too continued to study the three in the distance.

'I think they are wearing war paint,' she repeated.

He nodded. 'I thought they were, but your eyes are better'n mine, especially at that distance. Do you recognize any of them?'

When she was slow to reply, he left off studying the distant trio and focused on her face. Her stunning beauty never failed to make him catch his breath, even yet. Her high cheekbones accented the perfect burnished copper of her skin. Her piercing eyes, even now seeming to dance with some hidden exuberance just beneath the surface, continued to look toward the far ridge. Her glistening black hair was tied back now, but its luster caught the sheen of the harsh Wyoming sun, bouncing it back softer, subtler, more mellow.

'Maybe,' she said at last.

He waited in silence, drinking in her beauty, even when he knew he should be watching those others.

'One,' she said. Her voice had changed. The word was less cautious, more relaxed. 'Blind Buffalo is very tall on a horse, and he rides like the one in the center.'

'Well, that's good news. They waitin' for us?'

'Wait*ing*,' she corrected, accenting the last syllable with exaggeration. Only the barest trace of a smile flickered in one corner of her mouth. Otherwise her face remained devoid of expression. Fallon laughed abruptly.

'Keep a civil tongue in your head or I'll beat you, squaw,' he growled.

For the barest instant she allowed herself a trace of a smile.

'You have taught me to speak my mind, my round-eyed husband.'

His easy grin contrasted markedly with her impassiveness.

'Yeah, but that doesn't count when you're correcting my English. I'm the teacher here.'

'A teacher should always provide the consistent example, my husband has taught me.' He struggled for an answer, but she saved him the trouble. 'Yes, I think they wait for us. They would not stay so long on the top of the hill, otherwise. They are too . . . too . . . They can be seen too well.'

'Too visible.'

'Yes. I could not remember the word. They are too visible there. We should go to them, so they do not have to stay there any longer. It is dangerous.'

Almost as if their minds were connected, they lifted the reins and nudged their horses with their heels. As the lead rope tightened their well-laden pack-horse tossed his head once, then lurched into motion and kept pace.

She rode a saddle much like his, rather than the blanket favored by her people. A colorful shawl was draped across her shoulders against the early spring chill, but beneath it she wore buckskins nearly identical to his. Both rode with a smooth rhythm that made them seem nearly one with their deep-chested horses.

Almost as soon as they began their course toward the waiting Indians the trio of warriors disappeared from view.

'They didn't waste any time getting out of sight,' Fallon observed, carefully accenting the 'g' at the end of 'getting'.

A small smile flashed across her face for the merest instant, but she did not reply.

They skirted the sloping end of a long hill to avoid the exposure of crossing its crown. As they did, the narrow valley came into view. In the center a copse of aspen trees offered cover from searching eyes.

'They'll likely be there,' Fallon said.

She nodded silently. She watched from the corner of her eye as Fallon slid a hand down and moved the forty-five in its holster at his hip, ensuring that it was quickly accessible. Then he did the same with the other one that he wore, butt forward, high on his left hip, just in front of a large knife.

Only by the faint ripple of the shawl which concealed her right hand could a watching eye have noticed that she did the same. An eye as watchful as that might have been stunned that a woman – an Indian woman – wore a white man's weapon in a white man's way. She wore only one, rather than the two he wore. Hers was, like one of his, on the left side, at the waist, butt forward. A knife rested in its sheath at her right hip.

Twenty yards from the aspen copse they reined their horses to a stop. Silence descended from the slopes around them, settling over them like a shroud. In that silence heel-flies buzzed around the horses' hocks. A distant magpie sent a raucous plaint into the brilliant blue of the sky. Somewhere in the trees a squirrel skittered across the ground, making a rustle only the keenest ear could hear.

They sat in the pregnant silence for several minutes. No trace of expression crossed either face. Each sat with a hand resting easily on the butt of the left-hand, butt-forward gun, but they emitted no other indicator of animosity or readiness.

Suddenly three Indians moved out of the trees, mounted on pinto horses. Two of them were sorrel-and-white pinto. The other was black-and-white. They appeared so abruptly that they seemed to have materialized out of thin air.

Neither Fallon nor the woman flinched or spoke. They calmly and slowly looked over the three.

The center Indian was large, even for a Shoshone. His broad shoulders and deep chest exuded great strength. The war paint on his face only accented the angular strength of his features. His eyes were as piercing as those of the woman. Each warrior's eyes flickered across her, then focused on Fallon.

It was Fallon who spoke, speaking in fluent Shoshone as he nodded to each Indian in turn.

'Blind Buffalo. Hides From Bear. Bad Leg Running. It is good to see old friends.'

Hides From Bear responded first.

'The woman I gave you looks well.'

'The woman you sold me,' Fallon corrected, 'is well. As I remember, you made me pay seven horses and a buffalo-skin for her. Such a price was never before paid for one wife.'

'If I would have known how much your heart would grow bonded to her, I would not have offered her to keep the bed of a visitor warm.'

'Or how much my heart would entwine with his,' the woman said.

The unexpected sound of her voice brought a sharp flicker across the face of all three of the Indians. It was more than their implacability could withstand that a squaw would speak, unbidden, in the presence of warriors.

'Now you make her like a white woman,' Hides From Bear accused from behind a tight scowl. 'I would cut a woman's tongue out for speaking without being asked.'

'I am a white man,' Fallon said slowly, carefully. 'Among my people, a wife is taught to speak her mind.'

'It is not good. Neither is it good that you will not share her, as a man ought to do. Even when you visit her people, you do not share her. Even with the one who shared her with you, you will not share. It is not good.'

Blind Buffalo interrupted the conversation.

'It is not a matter of this day.'

Just as eager as Blind Buffalo to follow a different track of discussion, Fallon leaped at the opportunity.

'My brothers wear paint. The Shoshone are at war?'

Blind Buffalo replied. 'Only we three. We set out to avenge a raid by some Arikara. There were seven who attacked to steal some horses. They killed two of the boys who were guarding them. One was my son.'

Fallon's lips pursed. 'My heart shares the sorrow of Blind Buffalo. Did he die as a warrior?'

'He fought well, for a boy. He left Arikara blood on the ground before he died.'

'Then you have pride for his courage.'

'But with great sorrow my heart is sick.'

'You have followed them?'

The big Indian nodded. 'We followed them. We found them. They are too many for three. The seven were only part of them. There are fifteen Arikara who have entered the land of the Shoshone. We will return for others, then we will find them and destroy them and get our horses back.'

Silence built a wall as Fallon tried to put the whole picture together. Eventually he decided to approach the subject directly.

'Why have you told us?'

Without looking at the other braves Blind Buffalo said:

'Hides From Bear still feels for the woman he sold to you. He does not wish the Arikara to have her. That would make his heart sick with sorrow as well.'

'They are following us?'

Blind Buffalo shook his head and motioned broadly toward the south.

'Over there, there are nine wagons of white people. They are two valleys south of here, in the same direction you were going. It is good that you should stay away from them.'

'Why? They are bad medicine?'

'They will all die. The Arikara wait for them.'

'That's a pretty good-sized bunch of folks for fifteen Arikara to attack.'

'They will not attack directly. The Arikara are like the coyote. They sneak. They pretend. They leap from hiding because they are cowards. They will find a way to trick the white people with the funny hats.'

'Funny hats?'

'They all wear hats that look alike. Flat on top, like they were stepped on by buffalo. Their women all wear hats too. Woman hats. Wrap around their face, over their head. All one color.'

'Ah! Quakers!'

'What are "Quakers"?'

'It is a people with a strange way of worshiping their god.'

'All white people do not have the same god?'

'It is the same god. They think God wants them to dress different, talk different from normal folks.'

'I believe they will bleed like all white people.'

Fallon nodded. 'I reckon. Unless somebody warns them.'

'It is their trouble.'

'But it would be good that they know.'

'It is not good to step into the troubles of another. It is not our concern.'

'It is not good to let them walk into a trap they do not see.'

'If they are to know, their god should tell them. We

11

have told you that you not die with them. Hides From Bear does not wish Arikara to have Bird Shadow.'

It was the first time any of them had used the woman's name. The oddity of a warrior actually speaking the name of a woman in her presence in such a way was not lost on any of them. Without a further word, the three Indians wheeled their horses and galloped out of sight toward the west.

They sat in silence until the trio was out of sight. Bird Shadow spoke first.

'You will tell them?'

He nodded. 'I gotta.'

'Have to.'

'I have to,' he acknowledged, without lessening the scowl that creased his face. 'It isn't right to let folks ride right into certain death that way.'

'My people would never understand that.'

'I know it. The same as I can't understand why your people would ride right on past someone dying of hunger, or wounded, or hurt, and never offer any help.'

'If it were one of our own tribe, we would help.'

'Yeah, I know. Other people's problems are their own problems.'

'My people cannot think of any reason anyone would interfere to help or hurt, if it did not involve any threat to them.'

'Anyway, we gotta . . . we have to see if we can tilt the odds a little.'

'I am becoming too much a white woman. It seems like the right thing to do.'

She didn't see his small smile as he wheeled his horse. They set off to the south at a rapid trot.

CHAPTER 2

He nearly fell out of the saddle.

'Yow!' he yelled. 'You two scared the livin' daylights outa me!'

A barest smile flickered across Fallon's face. Bird Shadow offered no expression at all.

'Seems to me a scout oughta be more careful.'

'Well, now, I thought I was keepin' a sharp eye out. You two jist popped up outa nowhere.'

'You're the scout for the wagons?'

'Yip. They call me Kip.'

Bird Shadow turned her face away suddenly. Fallon merely hid his amusement at the sound of the statement behind the lush growth of his bright-red beard. The scout continued. 'My name's Ezekiel Kipperson. Kip's a mite easier to say.'

Fallon nodded. 'They're headin' for trouble.'

'Who?'

'You. The wagon train. The Quakers.'

Kip frowned. He backed his horse carefully, making it look as if the animal were merely shifting its feet. He wanted a little more room to maneuver, if necessary. His hand slid down close to the butt of his gun.

'How do you know that?'

Fallon ignored the question. 'There's a band of Arikara braves pullin' off raids on the Shoshoni. This is Shoshone country. They've got their eye on that wagon train.'

'How do you know that?'

'Some of my wife's people warned us not to stray too close.'

'Why would they do that?'

' 'Cause she's Shoshone,' was all the answer Fallon was inclined to offer.

Kip studied him carefully. 'They don't seem hostile.'

Surprise lifted Fallon's bushy red eyebrows.

'You've talked with 'em?'

Kip nodded. 'They showed up jist as we was breakin' camp the day afore yesterday. There's seven of 'em. They wanted some food. Said they hadn't eaten fer three er four days.'

'So the folks fed 'em?'

'Sure. They wouldn't never turn anyone away hungry.'

'So they had the chance to count your guns and figure out the best way to attack your camp.'

'What?'

'They weren't hungry. The timber's full of game. They were sizing you up.'

Kip's doubt was evident on his face.

'Well, I don't know. Yeah, game's plumb plentiful this year. Still, they seemed plumb friendly. I know enough Sioux we could talk purty fair.'

'There are fifteen of them.'

'What? Fifteen? No. Just seven.'

14

'That's what I'm tryin' to tell you. There are fifteen in the band. Those seven are just the scouts, sizing you up.'

'I'm havin' trouble buyin' that. They even told us a couple great spots to camp.'

'They told you where to camp?'

'Sure 'nough. The spot they told us about last night was well nigh the finest campsite we'd found since we left the Missouri. I 'spect the one tonight'll be jist as good.'

'Where is it?'

'About three miles further on than where they're at now. Nice flat spot, with a spring. Hills ringin' it all around, so no wind'll bother. Good grass fer the cattle an' horses. Room fer the kids to run an' play.'

Bird Shadow's words were both unexpected and harsh. They sounded as if she were spitting each word out individually.

'And a perfect spot to put rifles on the hills and have you completely surrounded with no place to run.'

A dark shadow settled across Kip's face.

'You know that place?'

She nodded. 'I know it very well. My people will not camp there without sentries around the whole circle of hills. If an enemy comes and you don't have those sentries, it is like shooting ducks in a small pond that has a net cast over it, so they cannot fly away.'

'Sounds like they're just leading you into a killing ground,' Fallon agreed.

The dark shadow over Kip's face gave way to an unnatural pallor.

'I gotta stop 'em, then.'

15

Before he could wheel his horse, Fallon held up his hand.

'Wait a bit. Let's think this through. If you stop them, or change courses, they'll probably attack you straight away. That'll cost some lives, sure's anything.'

'Yeah, but they said they'd come see us in camp tonight. That means there'll be some of 'em inside o' camp, an' the rest on the ridge all around us. We won't have a chance if you're right about 'em.'

'We're right about 'em,' Fallon assured him. 'Ain't no doubt on that. An' that whole wagon train full of people is about to be in a whole peck o' trouble.'

They both frowned, staring into the distance, seeking some hidden solution. At last Fallon turned to Bird Shadow.

'You got any ideas, Bird Shadow?'

She nodded slowly. 'At one side of that hollow place, there is a place big enough for the wagons to circle. It is not by the spring, so it would not be the natural place they would expect you to camp. It is out of good rifle range from the ridge on the far side. That would leave only one ridge to protect against. You could take one or two men with you, hide on that ridge, and be ready when the Arikara come. They will not expect you there.'

Fallon turned his attention back to Kip.

'Will Quaker men fight?'

'Oh, they'll fight, all right enough, if they know they sure 'nough gotta. They won't lift a hand agin' nobody till they know it's life er death, though.'

'Then take at least two with you. Take men who won't hesitate to shoot. Make sure they're well hidden. Tell

16

them what'll happen. You be in the center, so you'll have the most important spot.'

Bird Shadow spoke up again. 'The Arikara who come to talk must be kept outside the circle of the wagons.'

'What?'

'You must have them make their fire outside the circle of the wagons. Make sure none of the Arikara are allowed on the inside of that circle.'

Kip pushed his hat onto the back of his head, scratching as though the unexpected concentration made his head itch.

'That makes sense. But if I'm up on the ridge, who's gonna make sure they don't get inside the wagons?'

'We will.'

'You will?'

Fallon nodded. 'Take us to the wagons. Introduce us. We'll ask to string along with them for a couple days.'

'You could get yourselves kilt.'

'That could happen. We'll try real hard to see it doesn't.'

After several more minutes' earnest conversation, Kip agreed. They rode at a swift trot to the lumbering wagons. The welcome from the group was open but cautious.

Following the introductions, Ian McGregor said:

'Dost thou wish to sup with us, friend? Thou'rt welcome, if thou dost.'

'Why, thanks,' Fallon replied. 'We'd be plumb obliged. The missus might even be able to offer your women a bit of advice on gatherin' some of the stuff out'n the woods thet's good fer grub, too.'

'I'm sure her suggestions shall be well received. Wilt

thou ride with us to the campsite we approach? There I shall introduce ye both to the others of our company.'

Kip spoke up. 'Yeah, about that there campin' spot. . . .'

'Hast thou a problem with it?'

'Yeah, as a matter o' fact I do. They's sign around of more'n jist them Injuns what been come inta your camp. Thet campsite's a spot that ain't defendable, if'n they're up to mischief.'

'Mischief? They have come as friends.'

'Yeah, I know, but things ain't exactly like they been sayin', an' I ain't sure they're as friendly as they act.'

'Thinkest thou their friendship is an evil ruse?'

'Well, now, I ain't right sure, but it seems plumb likely.'

Ian shook his head. 'It runneth contrary to our teachings to think evil of another without proof. "Love believeth all things," the Scriptures saith.'

Kip replied instantly. 'Scripture also says that "Satan appeareth as an angel of light." These folks have purty good reason to believe Satan's usin' these Arikara to destroy a wagon train o' godly Quakers.'

Ian's indecision was obvious. Kip hastened to make his point. 'They's a spot that'll accommodate the wagons off to the side o' thet clearin', jist under one ridge that'd be a heap safer'n circlin' 'em right by the spring. The women'll have to carry water a ways, but it'll be outa range o' folks on the other ridges. I'd like ta have another man er two with me on the ridge right above the wagons fer the night, too, jist in case they got something in mind.'

'Thou'rt of a right suspicious of mind, Ezekiel. Hast

thou basis for this suspicion?'

'I know how to read sign,' Kip responded, without telling the source of his information. 'Thet's why ya hired me. It's the sign making me right suspicious.'

'But our new friends from among our red brethren have, so far, proved themselves faithful to their word. Last night's campsite was exactly as they presented unto us.'

'Yep. It was that. But I'd sure like to err on the safe side nohow. The sign all says they're dealin' a crooked hand.'

'A crooked hand? Dost thou make reference to some form of gambling?'

'Yeah. It means everything ain't like it seems. You'd be well advised to meet 'em ta palaver outside the wagon circle, too. They'll likely come up with all sorts o' reasons to get into the circle, where you cain't shoot at 'em without shootin' each other. Ya gotta make sure ya meet 'em at a special fire, between the wagons an' the spring.'

Ian frowned. 'How would I explain that breach of courtesy to them that have presented themselves as friends unto us?'

'You don't need to explain it. Jist be sure ya do it. Jist tell 'em that there's where you're gonna palaver. Oh, an' Fallon an' Bird Shadow here'll help out some. They kin take my place in talkin' with 'em. I'll be up on the ridge with a couple o' the boys.'

Ian frowned deeply. He studied his guide, Fallon, and Bird Shadow in turn for several minutes. The conflict spread itself across his face clearly as he pitted his trust of the scout against the tenets of his faith and his instinctive trust of human nature. At last he squared his shoulders. His words were stiff.

'Very well, Ezekiel. We will do as thou sayest. Thou mayest have Isaiah Smith and Thomas Wilson to accompany thee. But if events prove thee to be wrong, I will expect thou wilt properly apologize unto our red brethren thou distrusteth so.'

'Fair enough.'

CHAPTER 3

Anger clouded the faces of the five Arikara Indians. A brightly dancing fire flickered shadows across food set out for their supper. Beside it waited four of the men from the wagon train. The aroma of roasting venison emanated from an improvised spit. Smells of other foods wafted enticingly from Dutch ovens nestled in the edges of the coals. Nonetheless, the wagon train's visitors were visibly displeased.

'Why are we kept at such a distance from our new friends?' the leader of the group demanded.

Fallon, interpreting now for the absent scout, translated the words to Ian McGregor.

Ian faltered as he replied: 'We, uh, that is, we, uh, decided thou wouldst be easier in thy minds if thou wert not interjected into the midst of the devotions that be our evening custom.'

Fallon, turning to the Indians, said instead: 'Because we do not know whether the Arikara come as friends or foe. Where are the other two who were with you two days ago?'

The Indians cast sidelong glances at each other, but their faces remained impassive. None of their hands was visible, except the fingers that held the blankets around their shoulders. Those trade blankets hung down loosely, so nothing of the Indians themselves was exposed except their ankles and feet below, and their heads above the blankets.

Attired in almost identical style, Bird Shadow stood half a step behind her husband, just at his right. Fallon himself stood openly in his buckskins, his two pistols and large knife clearly visible.

The four men from the wagon train were without weapons, preferring their Quaker message of pacifism and acceptance to be clearly projected to their guests. Fallon kept two steps away from the four, positioned to face the five Indians squarely.

Ignoring the query about the missing pair, the leader of the Arikara replied:

'Have we not shown our new friends fine campsites?'

Without turning his head, Fallon said in English:

'He wants to know if the campsites they told you about were good.'

'Thou mayest tell him the campsites have been all that he said they would be.'

Fallon translated the wagon master's words accurately that time.

'Why are the wagons now circled so far from the spring?' the Indian pursued. 'It is far for the women to carry water.'

'He wants to know why you put the wagons so far from the spring,' Fallon relayed.

'Thou mayest tell him merely that site seemeth more well chosen, in case of an attack.'

Fallon did so.

22

He did not miss the furtive glances that passed again between the Indians.

'Who would attack?' demanded the leader. 'If there were enemies within the area, we would have certainly warned our new friends of their presence.'

Without waiting for the wagon master's response, Fallon said:

'What if you were the enemy?'

Each of the Indians stiffened. Hands moved beneath each blanket, but nothing else was visible.

'If we were an enemy, why would we show ourselves in peace?'

Again Fallon did not interpret or wait for a response.

'Maybe to set things up for the other ten Arikara who are on a war party against the Shoshone.'

As if on some unheard signal, the five Indians dropped the blankets that shrouded them. Three of them held now-exposed rifles. The other two held bows, to which they swiftly nocked arrows.

Gasps of surprise and fear issued from the lips of the four men from the wagon train as they realized that they were unarmed and helpless in the face of foes whose intentions were now obviously less than honest and far from friendly.

Events unfolded more quickly than the eye could follow. Dropping her own blanket, Bird Shadow thrust a large, cumbersome-looking weapon forward, even as Fallon's hand reached for it. There was an instant of hesitation as the Indians saw it. It was clear none of them had seen its like before, nor had any inkling of its fearsome fire power.

Their instant of surprise and hesitation was sufficient. Fallon did not hesitate. Grasping the Colt revolving shotgun pointed forward at waist level, he began firing as rapidly as he could squeeze the trigger.

At each squeeze of that trigger, the gun roared, sending a load of buckshot into the middle of one of the party of Indians, then moving just as quickly to center on the next as the gun roared its message of swift and violent death.

Four of the five were thrown violently backward by that blast of buckshot. As the strange gun centered on the fifth, Fallon held his fire. That fifth of the foes was already falling. Glancing sideways he saw the forty-five in Bird Shadow's hand. A wisp of smoke trailed lazily from its barrel.

Dirt kicked up from the ground twenty yards in front of Fallon and the rest. An instant later the report of a rifle from the distant ridge reached their ears. It was followed instantly by a ragged volley of rifle fire. The bullets all fell short, but drew steadily nearer as the remote riflemen gauged the range and adjusted their sights.

The four men from the wagon train stood transfixed, as if unable to fathom what was happening. Fallon yelled at them.

'Get to the wagons! Take cover! The others are coming! We're under attack!'

Even then it did not seem to register. Fallon grabbed Ian by the shirt and spun him around. Kicking him in the backside, he yelled again: 'Get to the wagons! Get your guns! Protect your families!'

Rousing at last from their stunned inaction the four sprinted toward the wagons, with Fallon and Bird

Shadow hard on their heels. As they lunged into the circle of wagons rifle fire broke out on the ridge directly above them.

Ian stopped, staring upward.

'What goeth on yonder ridge? What meaneth that rifle fire?'

Fallon grinned, even as he sought cover.

'I reckon your scout and them other fellers jist surprised some Arikara that was gettin' ready to shoot fish in a barrel.'

From the far ridge a series of war whoops and shouts drifted in the hot, dry air. A smile passed across Bird Shadow's face and was gone. Fallon didn't miss it.

'Shoshone?' he asked.

She nodded.

'Wilt thou tell me what passeth?' Ian demanded.

Unlike his wife, Fallon let his elation show in a broad grin.

'Well, I reckon some friends of my wife jist surprised the Arikara over on thet ridge, where they thought they was gonna pick off a passel of you folks. I'll be plumb surprised if they don't ride in here directly with a few fresh scalps a-danglin'.'

Ian looked at the mountain man as if he were some previously unknown freak of nature.

'Thou wouldst rejoice at the savaging of human life and desecration of victims' bodies in such a barbaric manner? Knowest thou not that violence begetteth violence? He that liveth by the sword dieth by the sword.'

'Sometimes,' Fallon admitted. 'On the other hand, the violence we meted out kept that violence from

25

happenin' to you instead. If'n we wasn't here, every man in this wagon train'd be dead now, an' them Indians would be havin' a party with your women.'

Ian gaped. 'I . . . thou canst not believe that human beings wouldst act in that depraved and savage manner. If thou hadst not challenged them, they would be eating in peace with us this moment.'

'If we hadn't challenged them,' Fallon argued, 'They'd have killed you four in the blink of an eye. Why do you think they were hidin' their weapons like that?'

When the wagon master failed to answer, he pursued it. 'Why do you think they had riflemen on the ridge over there, and up here both? If you'd camped where they planned for you to, they could have picked you all off like rabbits. An' where do you think the other two was that come into camp before? If I ain't mistakin', they're hunkered down in the brush over by the spring, where they was figgerin' on surprising you from point-blank range.'

Ian's eyes darted to the trees and brush surrounding the spring. As if on cue, two Indians broke from cover, sprinting toward a clump of tall brush 200 yards away. On their heels a Shoshone warrior on horseback broke from the trees. Overtaking one of the fleeing Arikara he drove a tomahawk into the top of his head, sending his dead body into a crumpled heap from which he didn't move.

Without slowing, the Shoshone continued toward the other.

The other Indian, realizing he could never reach his hidden horse in time, wheeled and lifted his rifle. Smoke puffed from its barrel, but his onrushing enemy never faltered. Before the Indian could lever another round into the chamber, the Shoshone's horse barreled into him, sending him tumbling head over heels.

As the Arikara brave struggled to his feet he found himself impaled on the knife of his assailant. He gasped and stared into the impassive face before him, even as his eyes dimmed and darkness overcame him. He didn't feel the deft strokes of the knife and the quick jerk of the strong hand that ripped his scalp from his head.

By the time that Shoshone warrior had retraced his steps and scalped the other Arikara whom he had killed, two other mounted warriors appeared, waiting for him at the edge of the trees. Without a word, the three rode slowly toward the circled wagons.

'Hold your fire!' Fallon barked. 'These is friendly Indians.'

Ian looked at him incredulously. It was as obviously difficult for him to accept that they could be friends, as it had been to accept that the Arikara had been enemies.

Just then Kip and the men with him returned to the circled wagons. The scout walked directly to Ian.

'Fallon was dead right, Ian. It was a trap all the way. They had five Indians crawlin' up to the edge o' the ridge where they could fire right down into the wagons. They meant to kill everybody.'

The blood drained from Ian's face as he realized the magnitude of the disaster so narrowly averted.

'What didst thou do . . . Didst thou slay them?'

Kip nodded. 'We kilt four o' the five. The fifth one got away, but I think he was wounded some. What happened here?'

It took a moment before Ian could compose himself enough to answer.

'We, uh, that is, thy friend here hast slain . . . he and his wife, they have slain the five who sought to deceive us. Other savages, some whom thy friend declares to be friendly, approach. They have slain others.'

Kip turned to Fallon. 'You say there was fifteen?'

Fallon nodded.

The scout began to count up. 'Well, thet's five you kilt, four we kilt and one what got away, that's ten. That still leaves five.'

Ian sighed heavily. 'We have witnessed the slaying of two others by one of these that approach.'

'Down to three.'

'Less than that, likely,' Fallon corrected. 'We heard shootin' along the far ridge, where we was gettin' fired on from. I 'spect Blind Buffalo and company probably accounted fer some more.'

He stepped out between two of the wagons toward the approaching Indians. They rode to within ten feet of him, then stopped.

Fallon eyed a total of five fresh scalps dangling from rawhide strings.

'Well, that accounts for all but one, I reckon.'

'You have killed the others?' Blind Buffalo asked.

Fallon nodded, replying in the Shoshone tongue in which Blind Buffalo spoke. 'We killed the five lying over there. The white men's scout and those with him killed four on the ridge above the wagons. One got away, maybe wounded.'

Blind Buffalo nodded. His eyes flicked to the dead

Arikara and back to Fallon.

'Will the woman of our friend count coup on those you have killed?'

'No. If you want their scalps, you are welcome to them. You are welcome as well to the scalps of those who lie on the ridge above the wagons. If you can track the Arikara who flees, you can go back to your village with all fifteen Arikara scalps hanging from your spears. It will be a day of great honor for Blind Buffalo, for Hides From Bear, and for Bad Legs Running.'

'I have avenged the blood of my son,' Blind Buffalo said. 'If we find the fleeing Arikara alive, he will be avenged even more fully.'

Fallon restrained the shudder that threatened to betray his understanding of the full import of the grieving Indian's meaning. Partly to hide it, he said:

'I believe you told us about this set-up so that we would interfere.'

For the barest instant he thought the Shoshone warrior would smile.

'It is a hard thing for three of us to fight against fifteen Arikara braves. My son needed to be avenged. Hides From Bear knows the mind of white men. He knew you would do so. I think he hoped maybe you would be killed doing so, and then he could have his woman back.'

Fallon eyed Hides From Bear, his eyes working to hide the twinkle that emerged in spite of his efforts.

'It is my sorrow that my friend Hides From Bear's bed must remain empty of the warmth of the woman whose heart is entwined with mine.'

Fire flashed briefly in the Shoshone's eyes, then they became placid once more. Surprisingly, he spoke in English.

'Perhaps there will yet be that hope,' he replied. 'Is your health strong?'

Fallon grinned. 'Fit as a fiddle, I'm afraid.' Reverting to the Shoshone language, he said, 'May my three friends ride in peace. There is food where the Arikara lie waiting to have their scalps removed. It is good you should eat before you ride after the fleeing one.'

Only the swiftness with which they complied betrayed their ravenous hunger.

CHAPTER 4

Well away from the wagons, Bird Shadow laid out a camp for herself and Fallon. It was backed up against a low cliff, in a hollow washed out by some prehistoric deluge. Thick brush around it made it impossible for anyone to approach silently.

She had unsaddled their horses, removed the pack from the third animal, and hobbled the horses to graze on the grass near the spring. Fallon had long since given up trying to help her. It was the custom of her people that such things were women's work, and it would disgrace her if her husband needed to help her accomplish it.

While she was doing so men from the wagon train had retrieved the bodies of the slain Arikara warriors, all now devoid of their scalps. They worked until they were drenched with sweat, digging a neat row of fourteen graves. They wrapped each of the corpses in a blanket and lowered them as if they were their own relatives.

Ian opened his Bible, and the rest of the men swept off their hats. He read:

'Fret not thyself because of evildoers, neither be

31

thou envious against the workers of iniquity. For they shall soon be cut down like the grass, and wither as the green herb. Trust in the Lord, and do good; so shalt thou dwell in the land, and verily thou shalt be fed. Delight thyself also in the Lord; and he shall give thee the desires of thine heart. Commit thy way unto the Lord; trust also in him; and he shall bring it to pass. And he shall bring forth thy righteousness as the light, and thy judgment as the noonday. Rest in the Lord, and wait patiently for him: fret not thyself because of him who prospereth in his way, because of the man who bringeth wicked devices to pass. Cease from anger, and forsake wrath: fret not thyself in any wise to do evil. For evildoers shall be cut off: but those that wait upon the Lord, they shall inherit the earth.'

When he finished, he said a brief prayer. The gathered men in chorus said, 'Amen.'

They replaced their hats and fell to work, filling each of the graves and mounding the dirt over them.

'Seems like a powerful waste o' time and work,' Fallon objected.

'It is the least we can do, to give a Christian burial to them whose lives our passing through this land hath cost.'

'They'd never a' done the same for you. They'd let you lie for the coyotes and buzzards. Besides, a Christian burial don't seem fitting for them as wasn't Christians nohow.'

'Nonetheless, it seemeth our duty.'

'Well, then I reckon you gotta.'

When their campsite was laid out to her satisfaction, Bird Shadow joined the women of the wagon train, to

32

whom she had already been introduced. While they were cordial to her, they were awkward in her presence.

By contrast, Fallon fit in easily with the men. He apprised them of the lie of the land that was in store for them in the next few days. Kip asked a number of questions, especially as to the availability of water, which he readily answered.

Conversation lagged after the obvious small talk had expended itself. Ian glanced at the rest of the men several times, then cleared his throat.

'Dost thou have a destination of thine own?'

'Whad'ya mean?' Fallon queried.

Ian frowned. 'Thou hast an Indian wife, yet thou livest not amongst the Indians, it doth appear,' he faltered. 'Hast thou desire to join thyself with us?'

Fallon glanced around at the obviously uncomfortable faces of the others.

'Why d'ya ask?'

Ian cleared his throat again.

'Thou art a violent man. Thy wife shares in thy violence. We have beheld her, in the manner of Samson, it seemeth, slaying Philistines hip and thigh with neither regard nor remorse. We are a peaceful people. The Society of Friends believeth not in violence any more than profanity or the drinking of strong spirits. We wish not our women and children infected with thy violence.'

'You sayin' you don't want me 'n Bird Shadow in your wagon train?'

Each man studied his own worn boots as though irresistibly fascinated by them. Again, it was Ian who spoke for them.

'Thou hast our gratitude for intervening to save us from the Indians who sought our lives and . . . things. We will not dispute thou saved some, if not all of our lives. Yet we must be faithful to him that called us to live in peace, and amongst people of peace.'

'So we're good enough to save your bacon, but not to eat it, huh?'

Ian looked offended. 'Thou'rt welcome to any of our food thou wishest to have! We will not withhold from thee anything we possess, if thou but asketh!'

'I didn't mean that literal-like. I meant, we ain't welcome to travel with you.'

'Thou wouldst be most welcome, provided that thou wouldst become as we are, forsake thy violence, thy vices, any grievous habits thou mayest have.'

'You want us to be Quakers?'

'Thou wouldst be welcome among us.'

'But only if we become Quakers.'

'We have forsworn ourselves from being unequally yoked together with unbelievers.'

'Well, I don't reckon me'n Bird Shadow's ready for that.'

'Then what wilt thou do?'

'We're homesteading.'

'Homesteading?'

'Yup. Already got it filed. They's as pretty a valley as you'll ever see about two days' ride south and east of here. We was on the way there when we found out you folks was in danger.'

'And are others homesteaded there as well?'

'Oh, yeah. There's twenty or thirty homesteads in the valley that's lived on already. We got one of the best spots there is. Ours controls the water that'll let us graze pertnear a thousand acres, over and above the homestead itself. The town of Boxelder's in the valley, too, so supplies ain't no problem. Town's got a couple stores, couple saloons . . . well, I don't 'spect you folks'd care much for that. They got a church, too.'

Ian framed his words carefully. 'Wilt thou be accepted there, thinkest thou?'

'Whatd'ya mean?'

'Thou hast an Indian wife. Some there be among whom thou mayest not be welcome with her.'

Fallon frowned. ' 'Cause I'm a squaw-man, you mean.'

Ian nodded. 'Some there be that would call thee that.'

'Well, we'll just have to deal with that as it comes, I guess.'

Ian cleared his throat yet again. 'Wouldst thou accept kindly a suggestion?'

'I'd listen anyhow.'

'Didst thou have thy woman in Christian marriage?'

'Me and Bird Shadow? No, we married by Shoshone customs.'

Ian looked slightly embarrassed, but continued resolutely.

'Perhaps thou wouldst be better received among thine own brethren if thou wast joined together with her in holy Christian wedlock.'

'You mean we oughta have a Christian wedding too?'

'It may stand thee in good stead.'

'Are you offerin' to do it?'

'If thou wouldst like. I am licensed by the Society of Friends, and can surely bless thy union with sanction that is both sacred and legal, if thou so desire.'

'Well, now, whatd'ya know! Well! Dang! Uh, let me go talk to Bird Shadow.'

He summoned her aside and explained the offer and the possible advantages. After several thoughtful questions, she agreed, and the entire company gathered around them as they exchanged vows. One of the women furtively slipped a ring to Fallon just ahead of the ceremony.

'It belonged to my mother. I am sure she would be pleased if thou wouldst have it for thy wife as thou plightest thy troth.'

At the end of the brief ceremony Ian spoke.

'By the calling of God, I pronounce thee man and wife. Wilt thou now turn and face the assembled company?'

They did so, and he said: 'It giveth me great pleasure to present unto ye, Mr and Mrs Kerwin O'Fallon.'

Nobody clapped. Nobody cheered. Instead a quiet ripple of approving sound shimmered across the assembled body of smiling faces.

As soon as the ceremony was finished they shared together in a meal that quickly became a celebration. A large number of housekeeping items were offered to them as wedding gifts. They declined them all, protesting that they had no way to carry them. Their packhorse was already loaded to capacity.

Later they made their way to the campsite Bird Shadow had laid out for them. Fallon was delighted in the foresight of his wife locating that campsite well away from the wagon train. Not many men, he observed wryly, are blessed with two wedding-nights.

CHAPTER 5

'Oh, my husband, it is beautiful!'

Fallon grinned broadly, his teeth framed by the red beard and mustache.

'Didn't I tell you it was the most beautiful valley you ever saw?'

'Where is our . . . home . . . home. . . ?'

'Homestead,' he coached.

'Homestead. I am sorry, my husband, I could not remember the word.'

'Well, you remembered the most important part. Home. Look up that way, at the head of the valley, straight below the big peak with the snow on top of it.'

'OK.'

'It's too far off yet to see any details, but it's just in the bottom of the valley, straight below that peak. There's no good farm ground above it, so it's not likely anyone will homestead above us. That gives us both sides and clear up the mountain to run cattle.'

The dancing of her dark eyes stilled for a moment, to be replaced by a deep thoughtfulness.

'I still am not at ease with the idea of owning land and cattle. We have talked much of it, but it is a way of

37

life that is too much different from my people's.'

'You'll catch on to it soon enough.'

'It will be good to have a place that is always where we live. It is much work to move. But it seems strange that I will live in a house with hard walls.'

'You're gonna have to learn to clean house, instead of just moving every three or four days, that's true.'

Her eyes were troubled as she studied the bright blue eyes that twinkled back at her.

'What if I cannot learn to do those things? Or to wear the clothes of the white women? Will you send me back to Hides From Bear if I displease you?'

Fallon started to laugh, but something in his wife's eyes stopped him. His own eyes grew serious, piercing.

'Bird Shadow, do you remember the words that Quaker preacher had you and me say when he married us?'

'They were strange words. I did not understand all of them. I had never heard of plight and troth.'

'Well, those aren't the really important ones. The important ones were: "until death do us part." That means that you're my wife as long as we're both breathing. I will never, ever send you back to Hides From Bear.'

'Or take another, younger wife when I get old and fat?'

He did laugh that time. 'Or that either. I'm gonna have a hard enough time puttin' up with one wife. Never understood how a man could deal with two or three.'

'Among my people it is good to have two or three to share the work. I would not want to share my husband

38

though. Maybe I am already beginning to think like a white woman.'

'You're gettin' there,' he agreed.

'Getting there,' she corrected.

He laughed again. 'Let's ride on into Boxelder. We gotta ... We have to buy us a buckboard, a team of horses, buy you a bunch of clothes, and a whole passel o' stuff.'

She looked thoughtfully at him as she folded her hands on the saddle horn.

'Do you have so much money to buy those things? We do not have much to trade.'

'Money ain't no problem,' he assured her. 'I been makin' a killin' on furs for more'n ten years, and saved pertnear every dime. That's on top o' them saddle-bags full o' gold we found with thet fella's skeleton. I figger we got plenty to buy lumber for a house, buy a herd o' cows to get started with, an' live plumb decent till we can start sellin' calves.'

'Do all white men have so much money to buy things?'

'Well, no. It's a rare thing, to be sure. The Good Lord just done blessed me, I guess. Just like he did with you. Never thought an ugly cuss like me would ever find a wife as pretty and good as you are.'

'The people at Cheyenne did not seem to think that way.'

He frowned. The pain she failed to conceal in her eyes hurt him more than he would have admitted. He scrambled to find excuses.

'Well, we hadn't been man and wife very long when we went to Cheyenne. You didn't speak hardly any

English yet. That was more'n a year ago, after all. And there were just people there that didn't take kindly to Indians.'

'Will it be like that in Boxelder?'

He studied the ground a long time before he answered.

'I don't know. I hope not. There will probably be someone, now and then, that'll bring it up. But once you get dressed up like the rest of the womenfolk, and learn how things are done and all . . . I don't know.'

'Will we have to leave, if they do?'

'Nope. We're done leavin' places. We got a homestead. We're gonna build us a house and a barn and corrals. Then I'm goin' over by Cheyenne and get a herd o' them red white-face cows. If folks don't like us, they don't have to talk to us. We'll be just fine.'

If his tone of voice failed to reassure her, her misgivings were certainly proved right in their first encounter in Boxelder.

'I'd like a room for me an' the missus,' he told the desk clerk at the hotel.

The desk clerk shook his head.

'We don't rent to no Injuns. Too many bugs an' such.'

Fallon leaned over the counter. 'The lady's name is Missus Kerwin O'Fallon. You wanta see a paper?'

He thrust the marriage certificate in the clerk's face. The clerk swallowed several times as he read through the names, the officiant, and the witnesses. He handed it back to Fallon.

'It ain't my idea. I got no problem with it. It's just the policy o' this here hotel.'

40

Fallon reached across the tall desk and grasped the clerk by the front of the shirt. He hoisted him up across the desk so his nose was inches from his own.

'Listen, you pimple-headed pencil-pusher! You take my money and give us a room key or I'm gonna hold you here while my wife starts takin' slices off of your nose, half an inch at a time. By the time we get to your lips, I'm bettin' you'll change that policy.'

Both were surprised by the calm voice of Bird Shadow. She had stepped up beside Fallon and now slid the large knife out of its sheath. She placed the point of the knife against the suddenly ashen face of the desk clerk. Adopting an exaggeratedly cultured tone, she said:

'Oh, Fallon, please don't be so brutal. Permit me the distinguished privilege of beginning with his ears instead. The pain is almost as intolerable, and it will allow me to have the pleasure of several more slices prior to reaching his lips. Oh dear! I do believe he's trembling! Are you trembling, my good man?'

The clerk was stunned by the ferocity of Fallon's actions and Bird Shadow's threats, driven home by the feel of the sharp steel against his face. Then he was flabbergasted by her precise English and vocabulary. She sounded more educated than anyone he had heard for many days, and the combination confused him so much he almost forgot to be afraid. For just a few seconds. Then the fear came rushing back. A trickle of water tinkled softly onto the floor behind the desk, directly beneath the dangling legs of the terrified clerk. The words gusted through his trembling lips.

'R-r-r-room five'll be fine! Turn me loose! I'll get you

41

the key! I don't want no trouble. Don't let her get started on me.'

Fallon released him so suddenly he grabbed the desk to keep from crashing to the floor. 'I'll be plumb glad to take that key, providin' my wife's willin' to accept your apology.'

The clerk grabbed a key and thrust it at him.

'I'm sorry!' he gushed. 'I didn't mean no offense. Honest. I . . . I . . . Welcome to Boxelder! You folks plannin' on stayin' long?'

'As long as we take a notion. How much is the room?'

'It's . . . uh . . . it's fifty cents a day.'

Fallon tossed two dollars on the desk. 'Here's for four days. We'll let you know how much longer.'

By the time they had transported the load from their pack-horse to the room, half a dozen people were openly staring at them. Doing their best to ignore the stares, they took the horses to the livery barn and paid for their care. Then they walked to the mercantile store.

A middle-aged lady turned from straightening a stack of dry goods when she heard them enter.

'Good afternoon! May I help . . . oh! My goodness!'

Her eyes darted back and forth from Fallon to Bird Shadow several times in the space of a second. 'M-may . . . Oh, my goodness! I'm sorry! You startled me for just a moment there. We don't get many . . . I mean . . . Oh, damn! I'm not doing very well, am I?'

Fallon laughed abruptly. 'Well, your chin's workin' all right, but the words are stuttering some.'

'I do seem to have a disconcerting effect on people today,' Bird Shadow said.

The lady's mouth dropped open even further than it

had been. Then she closed it with a snap. She giggled with embarrassment.

'Oh, my goodness!' she said for the third time. 'I am sorry. May I help you?'

'Well, yes, now that you manage to ask.' Fallon grinned.

'I'm sorry!' the lady said again. 'My name is Jane Bloomenthal. My husband and I own this store. I'm not usually such a tongue-tied idiot. Honest! How can I help you?'

'My name's Fallon,' he offered. 'This is my wife, Bird Shadow.'

'Bird Shadow! Oh, such a beautiful name! You are married?'

'Yes, ma'am. Well, we've been married by Shoshone ways for quite a while, but we were married by a Quaker preacher too. Christian wedding. This is Mrs Kerwin O'Fallon.'

'I like Bird Shadow better,' Jane responded. 'No offense, but it's a much prettier name. Now what would you like?'

'Well, we got a homestead up at the head o' the valley. But we need some clothes for the missus, and a bunch o' stuff.'

Jane started to speak, then stopped. Her embarrassment and uncertainty were obvious.

'I . . . oh my goodness! Here I go again. I, well, I must just ask. Bird Shadow, am I to understand that you have never worn, uh, that is. . . ?'

Bird Shadow looked closer to blushing than Fallon could ever remember. She glanced at him, then back at Jane.

43

'I . . . I have never worn any white woman's garments at all,' she confessed. 'I have absolutely no idea where to begin.'

'But you speak such perfect English!' Jane explained. 'However did you learn to speak so well?'

'My husband has been a good teacher.'

'A good teacher is nothing without a good student,' Jane asserted. 'You are obviously a most intelligent young lady. Well. You will need to buy cloth and things here, and then you will need a good seamstress to make them into clothes for you. I know just the lady who would be wonderful at it.'

'Would she be able to instruct me in how to make them as well?' Bird Shadow inquired.

'Oh my goodness, yes! She would be delighted. I wouldn't be surprised, though, if she wanted you to teach her to make some things as well. She told me once she would love to be able to make moccasins, but didn't have the least idea how.'

'That would be a good thing.'

Jane turned to Fallon. An impudent smile played at the corners of her mouth as she spoke with exaggerated formality.

'Well, then. May I suggest, Mr O'Fallon, that you go find something with which to amuse yourself. Your wife and I have woman things to discuss, and we certainly don't want you standing here listening.'

Swift panic skittered across Bird Shadow's face before it reverted to the inscrutable mask Fallon knew so well.

'Is it necessary that my husband leave?'

'Oh, my goodness, yes!' Jane assured her. 'But don't

44

you worry about it. Ellen Shoemaker is a wonderful lady, as well as an expert seamstress. You will absolutely love her. Now you run along, Mr O'Fallon. Oh, but do come over for supper, won't you? We will expect you at seven o'clock. Not a minute before. We have a great deal of work to do.'

Fallon looked back and forth between his wife and Jane several times. The panic in his wife's face worried him, but the open friendliness of Jane's own expression allayed his fears for him.

'Well, I 'spect that'll be all right. Uh . . . I don't know where to go to at seven, though.'

Jane emitted a high, lilting, musical laugh.

'Oh my goodness! Of course you don't! Emmet and I live one street down, turn left at the corner, and we're the sixth house on your right. It's a white house with blue trim. The only one in town with blue trim, so you can't miss it. But not a minute before seven!'

Fallon turned to Bird Shadow. 'Well, I guess you do need to talk about a lot of woman stuff, so I'll work on linin' out a buckboard an' stuff for us.'

'Ralph Flannigan is the buggy-maker,' Jane offered. 'He's two blocks down on the same side of the street. He has good wagons.'

Fallon sidled toward the door, suddenly frantic to get out of there, to stop feeling like a fly in the cream jar.

'Thank you, ma'am. I'll, I'll see you at seven. Bird Shadow. Ma'am.'

He almost tumbled out the door. He stopped and took a long, deep breath. A shudder ran through him.

'Been outa civilization too long,' he muttered.

CHAPTER 6

As chance would have it, the buggy-maker had a buck-board to hand that was precisely what Fallon had hoped for. From the buggy-maker he was directed to a horse-trader, from whom he purchased an exceptional team of matched black Morgans.

He still had an hour to kill before he was due at the Bloomenthals' house. He tied up the team at a hitch rail and stood on the sidewalk, surveying the town. He idly swatted at a fly buzzing around his face. He scratched his backside, and eyed the saloon boasting a sign ONE EYED JACK'S.

He took half a dozen steps off the sidewalk into the street, heading toward the saloon. The thought of showing up at Bloomenthal's with whiskey on his breath brought him up short. A voice from the sidewalk he had just left turned him back.

Two men stood on the board sidewalk. One leaned casually against a post supporting a wooden awning. It was he who spoke.

'What happened, Squawman? Lose your squaw, er jist rent 'er out fer a spell?'

The man's companion laughed harshly, but the

laugh was cut short. With lightning speed, Fallon's hand whipped from his belt, then upward in a high arc. The large knife from its sheath at his belt seemed, as if by magic, to impale itself in the post the speaker leaned against. A piece of his ear clung to the blade.

His eyes widened as he jerked erect, his hand darting to his ear. Jaw gaping, he brought his hand down and looked at the blood on it, then grabbed his ear again. His eyes darted from Fallon to the knife quivering beside him, then back to Fallon.

'You . . . you . . . whatd'ya think you're doin? You coulda killed me! You cut my ear!'

'You call me a squaw man in that tone o' voice one more time an' I'll do more than cut your ear.'

The man's hand dropped to his gun butt. His companion moved a step to the left, brushing his own gun butt with his hand. All earth seemed to stop in hushed silence. Seconds ticked past with ponderous sluggishness. The man swallowed, his Adam's apple bobbing visibly.

'You . . . I oughta. . . .'

'If you oughta, you're welcome to give 'er a try,' Fallon responded.

The man swallowed again. He glanced sideways at his companion, noting the waxy pallor of his skin. His eyes flicked back to Fallon, obviously weighing his chances and not liking the odds. He opened his mouth, then closed it again. He wheeled and walked swiftly away. His companion backed two steps, then spun around and followed.

Tension drained from Fallon in a long sigh. He stepped up on the sidewalk and pulled the knife from the post. He carefully wiped all traces of blood from it and returned it to his belt.

'Now that was as impressive as anything I've seen for a while.'

Fallon started, turning to see the speaker he hadn't heard approach. The newcomer chuckled and spoke again. 'Sorry to spook you. I didn't mean to sneak up on you like that.'

'Guess I'm a mite jumpy,' Fallon observed, noting the badge on the other's vest. 'You the town marshal?'

The newcomer nodded as he thrust out a hand.

'That I am. Hal Walker.'

Fallon took the hand and returned the viselike grip customary to the greeting.

'Name's Fallon. Did I just break a law or two?'

Hal chuckled again. 'Well, now, I don't rightly know. If Fred was to press charges, I suppose I'd have to consider it. He won't. He's mostly hot air. You're new around here.'

Fallon nodded. 'Got a homestead up the valley.'

Recognition flickered in the depths of Hal's eyes, but his expression didn't change. 'Last one up, at the base o' the mountain?'

'That's the one.'

Hal looked him up and down.

'I knew it was filed on. Wondered when somebody'd be movin' onto it. You a family man?'

'Got a wife. No kids. Not yet, anyhow.'

'That so? Been married long?'

'Well, that depends, I guess. Been married some over a year, by our reckoning. Just married by a preacher less'n a month ago.'

49

Hal frowned in confusion, but said nothing, so Fallon explained. 'My wife's Shoshone.'

Understanding washed across Hal's face.

'Ah, I see. Is that what this little shindig was about?'

Fallon nodded. 'He was raggin' me some. Called me a squaw man. Somehow, the way he said it, it didn't set good. I figgered maybe I'd let 'im know that.'

Hal laughed abruptly. 'Well, I guess you let him know. I thought I was going to have to interfere to keep it from turning into gunplay for a minute.'

'I thought it might go that way myself for a little bit there.'

'You aim to earmark everyone in the valley that calls you a squaw man?'

Fallon looked deep into the marshal's eyes, then both ways up and down the street as he considered his answer.

'I don't rightly know. I know we're sure to get some words tossed at us for a while, till folks figure out her being Indian don't make no difference. I guess I hadn't really thought about how to handle it.'

'Honey catches more flies than vinegar, you know.'

'That's a fact. Still, I can't be lettin' folks bad-mouth my missus any time they take the notion.'

Hal nodded. 'Like you said, it'll be a problem for a while. Just don't let it get to be my problem. Where's the missus now?'

Fallon waved a hand in the general direction of Bloomenthal's.

'She and the lady from the mercantile store went off to see a dressmaker.'

Hal smiled. 'Jane Bloomenthal took her under her

wing, did she?'

Fallon returned the grin. 'Now that's as apt a figure of speech as you could come up with. Just like an ol' mother hen, she did. When she figured out Bird Shadow hadn't never had any white woman's clothes, she just plumb took over, handed me my walkin' papers, and told me not to show up at the house afore seven.'

'That sounds like Jane. Unless I miss my guess a mile, your missus has six or eight women friends in town by now. Does she speak English?'

Fallon nodded vigorously. 'Oh, you bet! We've worked hard on that. I didn't want her soundin' like she was ignorant. She talks like she just got out of one o' them finishin' schools back East.'

'Is that so? Then I take it you're an educated man yourself.'

'William and Mary College, as a matter of fact.'

'You don't say! Came West instead of being a Virginia gentleman, huh?'

'Yup. Now I hope you don't ask me to explain why.'

'No need. I grew up in Boston.'

'Is that a fact. One o' them damn Yankees, huh?'

Hal chuckled. 'You don't exactly sound like a Southerner yourself.'

Fallon chose not to pursue the matter any further.

'Is there some decent hands around a man could hire, that you know of?'

'What are you looking for?'

'Well, I'm gonna need a bunch o' help gettin' a house an' barn built. Bunkhouse, too, I 'spect. I plan to freight in cut lumber for 'em.'

'You're homesteading a lot different from the rest of the valley. Not many have the ability to do that.'

'We're plumb fortunate thataway. Got enough money to get the buildin's put up, then I plan on bringin' in a small herd o' them red white-face cows. I saw some of them over by Cheyenne, and they sure got a lot of beef on 'em. Anyway, I need some hands to build the house and barn, so we can get it done afore winter.'

Hal nodded. 'You're a lucky man. Virgil Whitson, from over by Casper, just finished up building that new saloon at the end o' the street there. He's got two men that work for him. He's sure enough your man. If you want, I'll introduce you.'

'I'd be much obliged.'

Two hours later, with arrangements for the buildings in Virgil's hands. Fallon's future was laid out more clearly than he could ever remember. He tied up the team and buckboard in front of Bloomenthal's house. Striding toward the door, he felt as if he had so much to tell Bird Shadow he would burst if he didn't get it told at once.

His knock on the door was answered by the most enchanting vision of beauty Fallon had ever seen. He took a step backward. The woman who stood before him wore a dress that spread from her slender waist to nearly brush the floor in a wide flounce. Her closely fitted bodice revealed a ravishing figure, then framed the face with a high collar of lace. The face was exquisitely formed, burnished bronze skin accented by high cheekbones. Her eyes were fathomless pools of dark mystery. Black hair glistened across her shoulders, its outer strands lying on her arms and reaching the elbows.

Fallon sputtered. 'Uh, pardon me, ma'am, is . . . uh . . . uh . . . Bird Shadow?'

As her eyes danced, Jane Bloomenthal stepped up beside her.

'Mr O'Fallon, isn't your wife the most beautiful creature you have ever laid eyes on in your entire life? Have you ever seen anyone so absolutely perfect?'

Fallon swallowed hard. 'I always knew she was a beautiful woman, ma'am. But I don't know how you could possibly . . . I didn't think anybody could make clothes that fast.'

Jane giggled. 'Oh my goodness, Mr O'Fallon! Even Ellen isn't that magical. She happened to have a dress she had made which hadn't been purchased. It fit Bird Shadow as though it were made just for her. Isn't it just darling?'

Fallon swallowed and spoke almost reverently.

'Bird Shadow, you are the most beautiful woman I've ever seen. If you weren't my wife I'd ask you to marry me!'

He reached out his hands to her, and she took his hands. Her eyes darted uncertainly toward her hostess, then back to her husband. It was clear she wanted to rush into his arms, and just as clear that deeply ingrained customs strictly forbade any such show of affection. Her eyes brimmed with tears at her indecision.

Jane stepped in with characteristic aplomb.

'Well, my goodness! Not all of her clothes will be this elaborate, of course. She will need much more practical working-clothes suitable for a rancher's wife. But a woman needs at least two nice dresses, too. They help make her husband appreciate her as a woman, after all.'

Fallon couldn't have agreed more.

CHAPTER 7

'Company comin', looks like.'

Bird Shadow stepped through the flap of their tepee. Her eyes followed the direction of her husband's gaze.

'One man, one woman,' she affirmed.

'Maybe some o' the neighbors coming to get acquainted.'

Bird Shadow did not answer. She looked around at their homestead. It all still seemed so strange to her, as though she had died and begun to live some different life.

The tepee was the only thing familiar to her. The large barn, already nearly finished, was completely outside her field of experience. Anything she had been raised with could be taken apart quickly and moved.

Even cleaning the tepee they lived in while awaiting their house was strange to her. It was a concept that simply didn't exist among her people. Whatever trash and garbage accrued from living in that confined space was left where it fell, or where it was shuffled out of the way. After a week or two, when it became too crowded, or the smell of discarded organic matter rotting became too great to bear, the tepee was simply moved to a clean spot of ground.

Now she had learned the art of sweeping. She had giggled incessantly as Fallon patiently taught her how to grip the broom, how to make the gentle strokes that moved the dirt and debris without raising too much dust. It was, after all, a dirt floor. But she had learned, and found she enjoyed the experience. She was looking forward to learning to do the same with a wooden floor. She had giggled at first when he told her the wooden floor would also require scrubbing. It took some time for him to convince her he wasn't just teasing about that.

She was far too reticent of her own feelings, yet, to tell Fallon what she looked forward to the most. She had heard all the stories he told her of beds. Until they had stayed at the hotel in Boxelder she hadn't been able to imagine what it would be like to sleep in such a thing. Then, when she experienced it, she felt as if she had died and were slumbering on a great, soft cloud. More than any of the new and wonderful things Fallon promised her, she looked forward to having such a thing of their very own. There she and her husband could spend their nights together in a level of comfort unheard of among her people.

There, perhaps, if they were so blessed some day, she might even deliver children. She sighed as her hand passed unconsciously across her flat stomach.

The couple approaching in the buckboard did not return the wave of greeting that both Fallon and Bird Shadow offered as they entered the yard area. Instead, they drove a wide circle around by the nearly finished barn. They frowned visibly at the sounds of a busy crew already hard at work. The man surveyed the complex of corrals already built. His frown deepened. As they stopped before the tepee their frowns turned to deep scowls. The woman pulled the shawl, thrown across her shoulders against the morning chill, tightly together at the throat.

'Mornin',' Fallon greeted. 'Get down and come in. Coffee's on. You folks had breakfast?'

Neither answered for a long moment. Eventually, through the scowl, the man spoke.

'I'm Luther Grimes. This here's my missus, Gertrude. We'd heard they was a squaw man settlin' up here. Didn't believe it. Ain't folks to spread gossip. 'Specially if we don't know it's true. Reckon it's true all right.'

Fallon made a visible effort to control his temper.

'We're the O'Fallons,' he said. 'My name's Kerwin, but mostly I go by Fallon. This is my wife, Bird Shadow O'Fallon.'

He put special emphasis on the word 'wife' and on the addition of the last name to 'Bird Shadow'.

Gertrude snorted audibly but did not otherwise reply. Luther leaned forward, resting his forearms on his knees, gripping the reins of the team.

'Fallon, is it? Well, let me offer ya jist a bit of advice. In all good heart, mind ya. You folks really oughta find some other place ta homestead. This here valley's all white. Lots of folks, includin' us, I ain't denyin', got some purty strong feelin's agin' the Injuns. We seen too much them savages has done. We ain't lookin' kindly on one of 'em livin' right in the middle of us. Her folks is gonna wanta come visit, most likely, then we'll be havin' stock run off an' our women won't be safe nowheres. It ain't nothin' personal, mind ya. I'm jist lettin' ya know. You're lettin' yourselves in fer a real hard time if ya try ta live here in this valley. They jist ain't no room for no Injun er no squaw man. An' puttin' up a bigger barn than any o' the rest of us kin afford ain't gonna change what ya both are. The quicker ya light a shuck outa here, the better off ya'll be.'

'And the better off the valley will be,' Gertrude's icy voice added.

Luther nodded in agreement with his wife. He lifted the reins and slapped the team into motion with a loud 'Giddyapp!'

They left the yard at a trot, dust boiling from the wheels in a low cloud that drifted away in the breeze.

Neither Fallon nor Bird Shadow moved until the buckboard was out of sight. Then Fallon reached an arm around his wife's shoulders and drew her to himself. She resisted stiffly, instinctively reacting to any physical show of affection outside, where even the crew working in the barn could see if they looked in that direction. Then her need for the comfort of his embrace overcame the reticence of a lifetime of conditioning. She turned to him and threw her arms around him. She kept her face buried against his chest, so that he would never see the tears she had not shed since she was a child.

'Now don't you go letting them upset you like that, Bird Shadow,' Fallon murmured into the glistening softness of her raven hair. 'There's bound to be folks like that, no matter where we go. But there's other folks, too. Like the Bloomenthals. Like the Shoemaker woman. Like that other couple we met in town. Why, we already got a whole passel o' friends in town.'

She wanted so badly to tell him she understood that, and agreed with it. But if she spoke, he would hear the tears in her voice. If she moved away from him, he would see them on her face. She would not be able to bear the shame of her man knowing she could not keep from crying, so she kept her face buried against his chest and hugged him fiercely.

She didn't know how much time passed that way before she felt the shift in his position. His arms, still encircling her, moved slightly. His face against the top of her head lifted.

'Someone else comin',' he said softly.

Panic surged through Bird Shadow. She relaxed her grip. Trying to dry her face unobtrusively against his shirt as she turned away, she turned her attention down the valley. Another buckboard approached. She furtively glanced at Fallon. Seeing his attention riveted on the approaching rig, she quickly wiped all traces of tears from her face. Only then did she look toward the approaching visitors.

'One man, one woman again. Not the same two, though,' she said.

'Well, thank God for that,' Fallon responded. 'I might be a mite outa patience with them.'

'Out of,' she corrected, 'not outa.'

He smiled but did not answer.

'Do you know them?' Bird Shadow asked.

'Nope.'

Fallon lifted a hand in greeting toward the approaching rig, and Bird Shadow did likewise. This time, to their great relief, the wave was returned. The buckboard approached them directly. The man driving it pulled the team to a stop.

'Whoa, Dusty. Whoa Ribbon.'

He wrapped the lines around the brake-handle.

'Howdy,' Fallon called out. 'Git down an' come in. Coffee's on.'

'Boy, that sounds good,' the man responded, as he climbed down from the seat. He walked around the team and reached a hand to his wife. Taking his hand, she stepped deftly to the ground, smiling at Fallon and Bird Shadow.

'I'm Ralph Cranston,' the man said, thrusting out a hand. Fallon grasped the hand, returning the warm strength of the other's grip. 'This is my wife, Martha.'

Fallon shook hands with her in turn, surprised at the strength of her grip as well.

'My name's Kerwin O'Fallon,' he said. 'Just Fallon to my friends. This is my wife, Bird Shadow.'

'Glad to meet you,' Ralph said, extending a hand to Bird Shadow. She took the hand and shook it firmly, suddenly overwhelmed at the thoughtfulness of her husband who had so carefully taught her this strange greeting habit of white people.

Martha reached out her own hand and the two women shook hands.

'Bird Shadow!' Martha said. 'Oh, that's such a beautiful name. Are you Shoshone?'

'Yes,' Bird Shadow responded, completely at a loss as to what to say next.

Allowing only a brief moment of the awkward

silence, Martha said:

'Oh, look at that barn! Oh, Ralph, that's the kind of barn I want some day.'

Ralph nodded his agreement. 'That's the kind we'll have, one day.' He turned to Fallon. 'You built the barn before the house.'

Fallon nodded. 'That's something my daddy taught me, from the Good Book. "Prepare thy work without, and make it fit for thyself in the field; and afterward build thine house".'

'Is that so? Never heard that before. You a religious man?'

Fallon frowned slightly. 'Well, no, not too much. Oh, I believe in the Good Book all right enough, but I never studied it like my daddy did. Anyway, we thought it made sense to get the barn done first, like it says. We're used to livin' in a tepee, so that ain't no problem till winter. The carpenter crew had their own tents till they got the barn framed up. Lately they been sleepin' in the barn itself.'

'I've never really been this close to a tepee before,' Martha offered. 'It's different from what I expected. It's really quite big.'

'Take Martha in an' show her what it's like,' Fallon suggested. 'Ralph an' I'll go check out the barn.'

That instant of panic passed across Bird Shadow's eyes, but vanished when Martha said:

'Oh, I would like that so much!'

As the women moved toward the flap of the tepee, Martha added: 'I've really always wondered how you could keep it warm in there without it getting too smoky. Do you leave the flap a little loose to let fresh air in?'

Fallon didn't hear Bird Shadow's answer, but smiled at the sound of her voice responding. He could hear the women's voices already chatting merrily as he and Ralph headed for the barn.

CHAPTER 8

'I had no idea there would be so very much to learn,' Bird Shadow lamented. Martha Cranston and Virginia Hostler both laughed.

'But you learn so quickly,' Virginia assured her. 'Your soap is just perfect. And it smells delightful! I never would have thought of squeezing all those wild roses that way, and putting the juice into the soap for those three bars you made for yourself.'

Ralph and Martha Cranston, together with Robert and Virginia Hostler and their two children, Winston and Constance, had arrived early that morning. The carpenters had asked for some extra hands to help that day, and it provided the women with the perfect opportunity to spend the day with Bird Shadow. The children had been sent outside to play.

'What do your people use for soap?' Virginia asked.

Bird Shadow giggled, surprised that she was so much at ease with these two women.

'My people would never think of using anything like soap,' she said. 'To be clean is not something worth any time or effort. It does not help stay alive in the winter.'

'But don't they clean up sometimes?'

Bird Shadow giggled again. 'For her wedding, a girl is washed. For that we use the white juice from the . . . soapweed! That is what it is called. She is washed and dressed in a clean white dress of very soft elk-skin for that.'

'You showed me that elk-skin dress you have,' Martha said. 'However did you make it that soft?'

'It is by chewing.'

'Chewing?' both women said at once.

Bird Shadow nodded.

'To make any skin really soft, like a dress, or like a shirt for a man you love, it must be chewed until it gets soft.'

Both women sat in stunned silence for a long moment before Virginia responded.

'I can't imagine doing that. Aside from the taste, which must be awful, I think it would be very hard on your teeth.'

Bird Shadow nodded. 'It is hard. Women do not have many teeth after they are old. They become worn down. A woman's work is very hard among my people. That is one reason a man needs to have more than one wife. It was hard for me, at first, to get used to living like Fallon was teaching me. To be so clean. To get rid of all the bugs. To—'

'You had bugs?' Virginia interrupted.

Bird Shadow shrugged dismissively.

'It is just part of life. To fight the bugs is too hard. I did not think anyone did not have bugs in their beds, and in their hair, and in their clothes, until my husband taught me. After we left my people, when he put all our things into an ant-hill I thought he had gone crazy.'

64

'An ant-hill?' both women said at once.

Bird Shadow nodded.

'If you put things on an ant-hill the big red ants that make those big ant-hills covered with the little tiny rocks – the ants will go all through them and kill and carry away every bug that is in them. They even take away the eggs the bugs have already laid, so there are no more bugs.'

'But then how do you get the ants out?' Martha asked.

Bird Shadow looked at her carefully, to be sure her ignorance was genuine. For just a moment she thought her new-found friend was making fun of her. She was reassured by the other's expression.

'They always go back into the ground when it gets dark,' she said. 'After the sun goes down, you can pick up your things and the ants and all the other bugs are gone. I did not know how much I did not like the bugs until I didn't have them any more.'

'I guess if you get used to them, maybe you just wouldn't notice them much,' Martha observed.

'Ever since I met you I have admired your hair so much,' said Virginia. 'It is so beautiful and so black. It's coarse, but you keep it clean and brushed so it shines so nicely. I just assumed you learned to keep it that way as a girl, growing up.'

'Life is very different with my people,' Bird Shadow said, feeling as though she was repeating herself. 'There is so much to learn, there is not time to worry about hair and being clean and things like that. I needed to learn the things I had to know to stay alive, to be a good wife, to take care of a family. I had to learn

65

how to gut a deer or a buffalo, which things, like the bladder, have many good uses. How to take out the sinews for sewing, which bones make good needles, how to sharpen them and make the hole for the sinew. How to turn a dead buffalo over to get the skin off, how to stake it out – stretch it – then how to cook the brains and rub them into the hide so it will not rot. . . .'

'Your men don't do that?' Virginia asked, aghast.

Bird Shadow giggled. 'Oh, no. That is woman's work. No warrior would ever do anything with what he killed unless he was away on war party or hunting party, too far to bring the women to work. It is a man's job to be a warrior. To fight. To hunt. To make weapons. To make babies. Not to do women's work.'

'Stay away from my husband!' Martha said. 'I don't want him getting ideas!'

They all giggled like schoolgirls, but Bird Shadow was learning and storing up immense amounts of knowledge about living in a different culture from that in which she had grown up. She was also learning how important it was to her to be accepted. The knowledge was especially precious because she knew that not all the settlers in the valley would welcome her.

Constance Hostler burst into the house suddenly.

'Mom! Winnie's chasing me with a toad! He says he's going to rub it all over me so I'll get warts and be ugly.'

Virginia rose with a long-suffering sigh. She stepped to the door.

'Winston! Come here this instant.'

It was more than an instant, but Winston Hostler shuffled around the corner. His heavily freckled face was downcast. He avoided his mother's stern glare.

'Aw, Ma! I was just funnin'. I wasn't really gonna rub it on her.'

His mother was unmoved.

'Winston, you are twelve years old. When are you going to grow up enough to stop picking on your sister?'

'I was just funnin' her,' he protested again.

'You'll think it's fun when I get you home! Now go get your horse and Connie's saddled. Mine too, since you don't seem to have anything better to do. Your father seems to be finished, so we need to be going.'

'Oh, all right,' Winston grumbled. Virginia turned back to Bird Shadow.

'Are you sure you're going to be all right here all by yourself? It's a long way, clear over by Cheyenne. After he gets there, Fallon will have to pick out the cattle he wants, hire hands to help him drive them back, and a herd doesn't move very fast you know. Especially since all the cows will have calves at their sides. He'll probably be gone a month.'

'I will not be alone,' Bird Shadow reminded them. 'The carpenters will still be building the bunkhouse. I have to cook for them. Wilma Whitson helps me. She has taught me how to cook many things I never heard of before.'

'She does seem nice,' Martha agreed. 'So does Bernice Haverscheid. It's good they could come and stay with their husbands while they're working on the place. I would think they'd be getting tired of living in the barn, though.'

'I've lived in worse places,' Bird Shadow said softly.

Both women looked at her, but she offered nothing

more, so they dropped the matter.

Half an hour later Martha and Bird Shadow stood together watching the Hostler family ride out of the yard. Before they were clear of the yard, twelve-year-old Winston challenged his ten-year-old sister.

'Hey, Connie! Bet I kin beat ya to that big rock the other side o' the crick!'

Without answering, Connie flattened forward onto her horse's neck. She simultaneously swept the short crop she carried into the horse's flank and kicked him with her heels. The horse responded by exploding into a dead run. She quickly took the lead, riding as if glued to the saddle, kicking the horse with every stride to coax even more speed from him. Winston pummeled his own horse for greater speed, but was obviously no match for either his sister or her horse.

'Robert, stop them from racing like that!' Virginia pleaded. 'They're going to get hurt.'

They couldn't make out Robert's answer, but no interference with the children was forthcoming.

When they were out of sight, both women turned back into the new house. Martha looked around at the sparse but new furnishings.

'You're really getting settled in nicely, Bird Shadow,' she observed.

'I am learning,' Bird Shadow agreed. 'Much of it is thanks to you. I am so grateful for all your help and advice.'

'It's the least I could do. I know what it's like to not fit in, not to be accepted.'

Bird Shadow studied her new friend's face, waiting. When nothing further was offered, she said:

'You have been like that too?'

Martha stared into space for a long moment, then sighed heavily.

'Actually, yes. I have. And I would be again, if people knew.'

After another long pause, Bird Shadow said:

'Knew what? Or is it polite among white people to ask such a thing?'

Martha smiled. 'You are such a strange person. You talk as if you were the governor's wife, but you don't really know even some of the simplest things. It must be very hard for you. No, it probably isn't polite to ask such a thing. But if I tell you, will you promise to keep it just between us?'

Bird Shadow's eyes were large, serious.

'I would never tell a thing a friend asked that I not tell.'

Martha sighed again. 'I need to have one friend I can trust with everything,' she said. 'Life is too lonely, otherwise. Anyway, I was not always a . . . good woman.'

Bird Shadow frowned, trying to make sense of the words.

'You . . . you were not good? I do not understand.'

Martha looked at her closely.

'Do you know what a whore is?'

'A whore?'

'Yes. Do you know what they are?'

'I do not know that word. I don't think I have heard my husband use it. What is a whore?'

'A whore is a woman whom men sleep with for money.'

Understanding lit Bird Shadow's eyes.

'Oh! *That* is what it is. Like the women at the places

69

they call the hog ranches.'

Martha nodded her head slowly. 'That is what I was, Bird Shadow.'

'You were a . . . whore?'

'Yes.'

'And you slept with men who would pay you money to let them . . . be with you?'

'Yes.'

'Does your husband know this?'

'Oh, yes. That's where he met me. He persuaded me that we could leave there, file on a homestead some-where where nobody knew either one of us, and start our lives over again.'

'Like Fallon and I are doing.'

'Well, yes. But everyone knows you're Indian. Nobody knows I was a whore.'

'That is a more shameful thing, for white people?'

'Wouldn't it be for your people?'

Bird Shadow frowned in thought.

'There are women among my people who will sneak around to sleep with a man she wants to sleep with, without her husband knowing it. But not for money. It is a shameful thing if a man will loan his wife to another man for money, but the shame is his, if he does that. It is not hers. If he did such a thing, he would never tell his wife it was for money. He would only tell her the man was his friend.'

It was Martha's turn to frown in an effort to under-stand.

'What do you mean, she would not know it was for money? Why else would a man let someone sleep with his wife?'

Bird Shadow's eyes studied those of her friend.

'It is different among my people. A woman belongs to her husband. It is of no consequence if a man wishes to loan his wife to a friend. It is no different from if he loans his favorite horse to a friend to use.'

'But what if she doesn't want to do that?'

'That is not her place to think about. It is her place to do as her husband tells her. It may be, as it was with Fallon, that she will very much like him. Or come to love him. That does not make any difference, if she does, or if she does not. If her husband says: "I tell him you will sleep with him tonight", or "this week", or "while he stays here", it is her place to do that. To tell her that because the man gave him money or whiskey would be shameful, but only for him.'

'How did you and Fallon meet?' Martha asked suddenly.

Bird Shadow shrugged. 'He became a friend of my husband. In winter, he came to visit. I was still new with my husband, but he gave me to Fallon anyway. Our hearts became knit together, and I did not want Fallon to leave, or me to have to go back to my husband. It is my great shame that I told Fallon what was in my heart, but it was in his heart too. So he talked with my husband. His name is Hides From Bear. Fallon paid very much to buy me from Hides From Bear. He paid seven good horses and a very fine buffalo-skin for me.'

'He bought you from your husband?'

Bird Shadow's eyes shone with joy.

'Yes. For such a price, he bought me. And then he married me, in my own village, so everyone would know

71

I belong to him now. But then we needed to leave my people.'

'Why did you need to leave?'

'Because my people can never understand that he will never share me with any of his friends. That is a shameful thing, among my people, that a man would be so selfish.'

'It's wrong for a man to keep his wife to himself?'

She nodded. 'It is selfish. It is unfriendly.'

'Not nearly as wrong as having to . . . be with men you don't want to be with.'

'That is a thing I am very glad my husband has taken me away from. It fills me with so much happiness to know that I will never be with another man except my husband, that I can just be his woman, and he will never share me.'

'Now *that* feeling I can understand better than you know,' Martha breathed.

CHAPTER 9

'I can ride as well as you. I could do the work of at least one cowboy. I want . . . I wish . . . I do not know which way is right to say it, but I would go with you.'

Fallon frowned. 'I know, but it ain't practical.'

'Isn't practical.'

He grinned suddenly. 'Well, there then. I'm so glad you agree.'

'I did not agree.'

'Sure you did. You said it isn't practical.'

'No, you said that.'

'No I didn't. I said that ain't practical.'

'And I only corrected your English, as you always correct mine.'

'But you still said it.'

'Stop making the conversation to go around in circles! You are making me angry!'

' 'Tain't nice to get angry with your husband.'

'It is not nice,' she corrected once more.

'See there? You agreed with me again.'

Her eyes smoldered. 'Will you stop that, and talk seriously about this?'

His own eyes lost the glint of amusement and

became serious.

'I am serious, Bird Shadow. I know you want to come with me. I'm not happy about being gone from you for that long, either. But one of us needs to be here.'

'Why? We do not yet have cattle to care for. The horses will not stray far from the horses of the carpenters.'

'Yeah, I know all that. But we do have a crew working on the bunkhouse. I don't think it's a good idea for both of us to just ride off for that long. There's no telling what folks like Plymouth and Henderson might do.'

Her eyes grew as serious as they had been angry moments before.

'Do you think they will . . . attack us?'

'If they knew nobody was keeping an eye on things, they just might. They're a pretty bad bunch, I'm afraid. I don't think they're brave enough to try anything with anyone here, but it wouldn't surprise me if they tried to burn the place down if there wasn't.'

Her eyes searched his carefully.

'You are asking me to stay here to protect our homestead?'

He fidgeted, suddenly uncomfortable.

'Well, I don't like saying it that way, but yeah. That's what it boils down to. And I want you to be careful. We got the dog now. He'll let you know if anyone's coming. If someone comes that you don't know, don't be afraid to meet 'em with a gun in your hand.'

She mulled the thought a long moment. The ghost of a smile toyed at the corners of her mouth.

'Then kiss me goodbye, husband.'

'You mean right out here in front of God and everybody?'

'Yes.'

He obliged, with relish. Then he stiffened with surprise, then with pleasure, as her tongue darted playfully into his mouth and back again. He held her at arm's length.

'What are you trying to do, woman? Make me forget about leaving?'

That smile twitched again, threatening to overwhelm her reserve.

'I am making sure you will return as soon as you can.'

'Well, that'll do it, that's for sure!' he grinned. 'You be careful, Bird Shadow.'

'You be careful too, my husband.'

It was the hardest ride he could remember, the first few miles. Everything in him tore at him to wheel around and gallop back to Bird Shadow. Eventually the urge retreated to a gnawing ache somewhere deep inside that longed for her presence.

He rode at a ground-eating trot, stopping only long enough to water and rest his horse. It was late on the third day when he trotted into the yard of the JH ranch of John Hunton, almost half-way between Fort Laramie and Cheyenne. John Hunton himself stepped out of the house to meet him.

'Well, I'll be dadgummed! How are you, Fallon? Long time no see. Get down. Come in.'

Fallon swung off the big chestnut gelding and stepped forward to take the rancher's hand.

'Howdy, Mr Hunton. It's been almost two years.'

'It has for a fact. What brings you down thisaway?'

'You remember those cows and calves we talked about?'

'Sure do. As a matter of fact, I held back last year and this, figuring you just might show up. I got a couple hundred head more'n what I oughta keep for winter.'

'That's what I was hopin'. They're what I came for.'

'Well, you said you would. I never doubted it. Come on in. You're just in time for supper.'

'That sounds good. I've been eating trail grub the last three days.'

It more than just sounded good. Blanche Hunton was not only young and beautiful – scarcely more than half the rancher's age – she was an exceptional cook. John introduced her and their two children to Fallon again.

After supper, as they enjoyed a strong cup of black coffee, John said:

'Tell me, Fallon, did you end up with that Shoshone girl you was so sweet on?'

Fallon sipped his coffee appreciatively before he answered.

'Yeah, as a matter of fact I did. I talked Hides From Bear into selling her to me. We got married there, then we got married again by some Quakers that come through. One of them was ordained.'

'Is that a fact? Well, more power to you. I had me an Indian wife once. Before I met Blanche. Did you know that?'

'Really? No. I didn't know that.'

'Yup. Sure enough. Well, she was half-Indian. Lallee, her name was. Sister to Little Bat, if you ever heard of him.'

76

'I've heard of him. French Indian.'

'Yup. Just like Lallee. Me'n her rode all over this country together. I don't know if I'd ever gotten over losin' her, if it hadn't been for Blanche.'

'I didn't know you'd been married before.'

'Well, I can't rightly say we was married. Not like me'n Blanche. We didn't have no Christian wedding, or nothin'. Couldn't, back in them days. There wasn't nobody in the country to do a ceremony if you wanted one. No, we just decided we belonged together, said so all around, and I guess that was just as bindin'.'

Fallon nodded. 'Bird Shadow and I were married in the Shoshone way, is all, for quite a while. We just chanced onto a wagon train of Quakers, or that's still what we'd have.'

'So what've you got for a place for these cattle?'

'Ever hear of Boxelder Crick?'

'Sure. Town of Boxelder, too. Crick comes down outa the mountains to the south and west o' the town. It's called Long Valley, if I remember right. Some fine country up in there.'

'None finer than ours. We homesteaded clear up at the head of that valley, where we can graze the high country in the summer and bring the stock down closer in winter. Plenty o' running water. Plenty of hay meadow right on our homestead acres, as well as on above it, so even if the country gets more settled, we'll have all we need. There really isn't any place on above us that would make a decent homestead, so we're sitting pretty.'

'Sounds great. Well, you're welcome to a bed in the spare bedroom. We'll head out at first light and start lookin' some cattle over.'

Fallon looked suddenly uncomfortable.

'Well, the fact is, I've been three days on the trail. I'm a mite gamy to be staying in the house. If you don't take offense, I'd be more comfortable in the bunkhouse with the boys, if there's a spare bunk.'

'It's your choice. You're welcome, either place.'

'I'm much obliged. By the way, how you fixed for hands?'

Hunton's eyebrows shot up.

'You aimin' to take some o' them from me too?'

Fallon nodded. 'If you don't mind, I'd like to hire three men to help me drive the herd. If they work out, I'll keep at least two of 'em on to put up hay and such. We'll be needing hands.'

Hunton nodded. 'I'm a bit long on help right now anyway. I hired a separate hay crew to put up feed for winter this year. With the stock gone that you aim to buy, I'll be a bit overloaded with help. You pick the ones you want. If they're willin', I'm game. I'll give 'em their time when you leave.'

The sun was just threatening to appear the next morning when the cook jangled the triangle to summon the hands to breakfast. As they finished the meal, Hunton walked in.

'Boys, if you ain't met 'im yet, the jasper in the buckskins is Fallon. He's here to pick out a couple hundred head o' cows and calves to buy. He'll be wantin' to hire three men to help him drive 'em to his place, a good two er three weeks north and west. Two of you can hire on there permanent, if you're a mind to. Those that choose to go can come back here and have a job anytime as well. For today, Russ, Joe and Had will ride with us. Flint'll line the rest of you out on what he wants done. We'll hold the critters Fallon picks out on the big meadow south o' the house.'

Russ Weathers, Joe Smith and Hadley Wright looked exactly the kind of hands Fallon was hoping to hire. Their work that morning convinced him further. The herd they looked over that morning impressed Fallon even more than he remembered. They were truly a fine breed of cows, and in exceptional shape. The JH brand graced the left hip of each animal. It was made so the upright line of the J and the left upright line of the H were in common. It seemed almost like a stamp of approval, placed only on the finest cattle he had seen in Wyoming.

Even so, he found it hard to concentrate. Some sixth sense kept gnawing at the corners of his mind, bringing up images of Bird Shadow. Twice he could have sworn he heard her voice, calling out to him. He grew increasingly edgy.

By mid-morning he spoke up.

'Mr Hunton, why don't you have your boys just cut out any two hundred head that have good strong calves at their side. I haven't seen a one that I wouldn't be proud to own.'

'Fair enough,' Hunton agreed. He quickly dispatched the three hands to accomplish the task.

'What about bulls?' he asked.

'You got half a dozen to spare that haven't bred any of the cows you'll be cutting out? I might want to keep some of the heifers to build up my own herd, that way I wouldn't have to get different bulls for two or three years.'

'That makes sense. You want red white-face bulls, or longhorns?'

'You got any half and half?'

'Yeah, as a matter of fact I do. That's what I'm shootin' for. I want three-quarter red white-faces and quarter longhorn. They're a little rangier, but hardier. They handle the winters better.'

'Sounds good. How much you want for 'em?'

'You want a hagglin' price?'

'Nope. They're your cows. You know what they're worth. You tell me what they're worth, and that's what I'll pay you.'

'In gold?'

'In gold.'

Hunton figured in his head for a few minutes, then gave Fallon a price. True to his word, Fallon only nodded.

'I'll count it out when we get back to the ranch.'

The morning sun rose on Fallon's new herd, stringing out along a trail that would take them to Long Valley. Fallon, with the bill of sale for the cattle safely in his saddle-bag, chafed constantly at the slow pace necessary for the young calves. The voice of that intuition insisted Bird Shadow needed him. He knew better than to ignore it, but he was helpless to get home any quicker than the herd could travel.

CHAPTER 10

Two days out from the JH Ranch, Fallon was increasingly edgy. He couldn't get Bird Shadow off his mind. His attention was jolted back to the present by a furtive movement along the crest of a ridge to his left.

His hand dropped instinctively to his gun. He scanned the ridge top carefully. Nothing moved. He moved his horse to one side of the herd and motioned to the hands who were busily keeping the cattle bunched together and moving steadily.

The three galloped to him.

'What's up?' Montana Smith asked. He was the only one different from the three who had sorted out the herd. Hadley Wright had chosen to stay on at the JH.

'I ain't sure,' Fallon replied. 'Caught a glimpse of something on the ridge. My guess is we're about to be greeted by some Indians.'

The three looked uneasily at each other.

'You think there'll be trouble?' Russ asked.

Fallon shrugged. 'Never know. It depends on what Indians they are. If they're Sioux or Crow or somethin', and a war party, then we could be in for trouble. If they're Shoshone they may try to talk us out of a cow or two, but they won't be a problem. We'll just have to wait and see. I just wanted you to be ready. You might ride with your rifles outa the scabbards, just in case.'

As if on common impulse, all three pulled their carbines from the saddle scabbards, checked to be sure they had a round in the chamber, and laid them across their legs.

'Want us to keep the cows movin'?' Joe asked.

Fallon nodded. 'Sure. Act like we ain't seen 'em. We'll just wait and see when they choose to make themselves known.'

They didn't have very long to wait. As the herd topped a low rise, five warriors on horseback were spread out in a line, blocking the way.

Fallon nudged his horse to a swift trot and rode to meet them. With confusion he noted they were Pawnee.

He raised a right hand in greeting. Instead of responding in kind, the Indian in the center nudged his horse forward to meet him. Fallon took the initiative, rather than waiting for the Indian to open the conversation.

'It is a long way west to find those of the Pawnee.'

The five Indians exchanged quick glances. Their looks became decidedly uneasy as the other three rode up behind Fallon, spreading out behind and beside him, rifles across their legs, their horses turned so the rifle barrels pointed toward the Indians.

'You speak well our language,' the group's leader acknowledged.

'I have long been a friend of the Indian,' Fallon replied. 'My wife is of the Shoshone. I am surprised to

82

see Pawnee in Shoshone country.'

The group shifted uneasily. 'I am Walks Alone,' the leader said. 'Our people live east of here, at the western end of the country of the Pawnee. Our game is scarce. We have come a long way to hunt, yet we have found no buffalo.'

'How many are you?' Fallon inquired.

'We are fifty,' Walks Alone lied. 'Twenty warriors with our women and children. We must eat.'

Fallon's mind raced. He knew the Pawnee was lying, but he didn't know by how much. It was almost certain that they were more than the five who showed themselves. That small a party would not have ventured so far into Shoshone country in search of game. Still, even half that number would exact a heavy toll if they chose to attack. He also knew that their need for food, verified by their gaunt frames, must be great to venture so far.

Fallon spoke over his shoulder.

'Boys, how many cows have lost their calves so far?'

There was a moment of silence, then Russ answered.

'Three, that I know of. One that got snake bit. One that drowned crossin' the Platte. One that the coyotes drug down.'

'Can you cut those three cows out without much trouble?'

'Sure. They're all three hangin' back in the drag, lookin' for their calves.'

Fallon addressed the Pawnee again.

'The Shoshone and the Pawnee have been brothers for many winters. It is good that one who has plenty should help one that has no game. We have three cows

83

who have lost their calves. We will leave them for our Pawnee brothers, that you may feed your women and children, and return to your village with fat stomachs. Then we will trust our Pawnee brothers to promise that we will go in peace on our way.'

The group of Pawnee were hard pressed to conceal their relief and delight. Walks Alone nodded.

'It is good.'

With no further discussion, the Indians wheeled their horses and galloped away. Fallon turned to his hands.

'Cut them three cows out and haze them over toward that clump of woods to the south. When they're about half-way there, just leave 'em and come on back.'

'Won't they follow the rest of the herd right behind us?' Montana asked.

Fallon grinned. 'I'm sure they will. For all of a dozen steps. The rest of the Pawnee are in that timber. They'll kill 'em and have 'em skinned before you get back to the herd.'

The three looked at each other, then back at Fallon.

'There's redskins in them trees?' Russ faltered.

Fallon's grin widened.

'Why do you think I was willing to give up three head o' cows? Now you best get it done before they get impatient.'

The three did as they were told. When they thought they were close enough, they wheeled their horses and raced back toward the herd. Not until they had caught up with the cattle and started them moving again did they dare to look at their back trail. Each of the three cows was hidden from sight by a group of Indians busily butchering the carcass. Russ shuddered.

'I don't know about you boys, but I'm plumb glad this guy knows Injuns.'

It was white men who proved the greater problem.

They were a week away from the JH Ranch, just over half-way to their goal. The night was calm, illuminated by a full moon. The cattle had time to fill their stomachs, nurse their calves, then settle down to chew their cuds and sleep. Far off an occasional coyote lifted his head and howled some lonesome message to his fellows.

Russ was on nighthawk duty, dozing in the saddle, completely at ease. He would have denied that his dozing had turned into sound sleep if Fallon hadn't wakened.

Fallon wasn't even sure what woke him. Something borne on the night breeze snapped his eyes open. He lay still, listening intently. He glanced at the moon, noting it was nearly three a.m. It took several minutes before he recognized a foreign sound at the far side of the herd.

Cattle were moving. They were not frightened. They were not running. But they were moving. They shouldn't have been moving.

He slid from his blankets. He moved to Joe and Montana in turn, touching them and whispering.

'Something's up with the herd. Saddle up as quiet as you can. Let's check it out.'

Both hands came instantly wide awake. They jerked on their boots and ran to catch up their hobbled horses.

Fallon was the first into the saddle. He rode to where

Russ sat, still snoozing in the saddle. At his approach, the cowpoke woke abruptly.

'What's up, boss?'

'You hear cattle moving?'

'Haven't heard a thing.'

'Listen!'

In a silence broken only by saddles that squeaked with each movement, Russ tilted his head, trying to pick up whatever sound Fallon meant. His head jerked erect.

'Over that way. They is cows movin', real quiet-like. What's goin' on?'

'Don't know,' Fallon replied. 'Either Indians or rustlers are tryin' to cut out a bunch o' cows without us hearin' 'em.'

The other two hands rode up, riding as quietly as possible.

'Whatd'ya wanta do, boss?' Montana asked.

'Let's have a look,' Fallon replied.

Riding at a trot, he led the way around the mostly sleeping herd. As they approached the eastern edge of the quiet cattle, the moonlight was sufficient to see several men on horseback.

'White men,' Fallon breathed. 'Rustlers.'

He kicked his horse into a gallop. The other three followed suit. Almost immediately one of the rustlers yelled something to the others. They began yelling at the bunch of cattle they had stirred from the herd and grouped a couple hundred yards away.

A streak of fire pierced the night, followed instantly by the report of a rifle. All four men bent forward over their horses' necks, presenting as small a target as possible.

'Hold your fire,' Fallon ordered. 'Wait till we're further from the herd. I don't want 'em spooked if we can help it.'

The rustlers were under no such compulsion. The night was suddenly alive with gunfire, all directed at them.

'Take 'em!' Fallon yelled, spurring his horse to a dead run.

A horseman appeared suddenly just to his right, raising a rifle to his shoulder. Fallon snapped a shot at him, and saw him jerk and fall from the saddle. He didn't slow.

He began to pass running cattle, abandoned by the rustlers. Several shots sounded to his left, followed by Russ's triumphant shout.

'Got one of 'em!'

A volley of shots to his right resulted in Joe's voice calling out:

'Make it two!'

'Three,' Montana corrected.

'Four, with the one I got,' Fallon told himself.

He passed the lead animals of the herd the would-be rustlers had tried to take. The moonlight was bright enough for him to see the tracks of two horses continuing onward. He reined in his horse. He called out.

'Joe and Montana, you boys round up these cows and get 'em back to the herd. There's still two in the saddle. Russ, you and me will see if we can catch up with them.'

He spurred his horse back into a long lope. Russ raced up beside him.

'Can you see well enough to track 'em by moonlight?'

'Easily, when they're running their horses like this,' Fallon assured him. 'I think one of 'em's hit. His horse keeps swerving, like he's swaying in the saddle.'

'You can see that in the dark?' Russ asked in awe.

Fallon didn't answer. He kept his horse at that long lope, the ground falling away swiftly behind them. Thirty minutes later he caught a glimpse of the pair, less than 300 yards ahead.

He didn't hesitate. Out of the corner of his eye he saw Russ pull his rifle from his scabbard, but he kept pace. The two raced side by side after the fleeing rustlers.

The duo realized that they were being pursued and urged their horses to greater speed. In response Fallon and Russ spurred their own mounts. They responded with a burst of speed, running flat out across the moon-lit ground.

The distance between them and their quarry narrowed quickly. The duo veered to the left, heading for a clump of cottonwood trees that marked a small creek. One of them swayed in the saddle. The other reached for him, urging him to keep running. They were close enough to hear him.

'Hang on, Slim! We make it to them trees, we got a chance.'

Slim tried. He simply couldn't hang on any longer. He slid from the saddle, landing in a crumpled heap on the ground.

Knowing there was no hope for his fellow, the rustler spurred his horse, leaning over the saddle horn, shouting encouragement to the tired beast. The noble animal gathered tired muscles to respond, but he was no match for Fallon's mount. In seconds the pursuer was alongside.

'Pull up or I'll shoot you outa the saddle!' Fallon yelled.

The rustler looked sideways, into the barrel of Fallon's pistol, and began to haul on the reins of his horse. As the horse had skidded to a stop, he threw up his hands.

'Don't shoot! I give up!'

'This one's a goner,' Russ called from where the other outlaw had fallen.

'Reach down and lift that gun out with a thumb and one finger,' Fallon ordered. 'Drop it on the ground.'

The man did so, careful to offer his captor no excuse to shoot.

'Now the rifle,' Fallon ordered.

The man complied.

Russ rode up beside them. Fallon addressed him without taking his eyes off the rustler.

'Tie his hands behind him, Russ.'

Russ pulled a length of rope from a saddle-bag and rode up on the far side of the prisoner. Being careful to stay out of the line of Fallon's fire, he quickly bound the man's hands behind him. Only then did Fallon holster his gun, taking the reins of the captive's horse.

Russ exhaled an audible sigh of relief.

'Now what, boss?'

Fallon ignored him and addressed the captive.

'What's your name?'

'Richard Davis.'

'Where you from?'

'Nowhere in particular.'

'Got any family?'

'No. Why?'

'Need to know who to notify.'

Even in the moonlight, Fallon could see the man's eyes widen.

'You aimin' to hang me?'

'That's what usually happens to rustlers, isn't it?'

The man stared a moment. His head drooped.

'Yeah. I guess it is.'

Fallon nudged his horse. The animal responded, heading toward the cottonwood grove. The captive's animal, responding to the tug on the reins, followed closely. Russ trailed along wordlessly.

No more was spoken. Fallon led the rustler's horse beneath a high, horizontal limb of a large tree. Russ whirled his rope twice and cast the loop unerringly up and over the limb. It hung down so the loop was nearly to the horse's rump.

Fallon grabbed the loop and dropped it over Davis's head, snugging it around his neck, placing the hondo to the side, just under his ear.

Russ pulled out the slack and tied the end of the rope to the tree.

Fallon backed his horse a couple steps.

'You got anything you want to say?'

Davis raised his head and looked first at Fallon, then at Russ, then back at Fallon. He started to speak, and his voice caught. He cleared his throat.

'The others all dead?' he asked softly.

Fallon nodded.

'Just get it done,' he choked out.

Fallon rode up behind the rustler's horse and

90

slapped the animal sharply on the rump. The horse lunged forward. Choosing swift death, his rider gripped the saddle as hard as he could with his knees. That jerked the noose instantly and severely tight around his throat. It dug in, shutting off his air, blocking the carotid arteries. Darkness came with swift mercy.

Neither Fallon nor Russ watched him die. Fallon spurred his horse and caught the outlaw's riderless mount. Russ rode to where the other dead man's mount patiently waited, reins dragging the ground. He caught the reins and led the animal along, following his boss back to the herd.

Only the moon continued to look down on the lifeless body, swaying slowly beneath the limb of a cottonwood tree.

CHAPTER 11

She was not a child! She refused to act like a child, incapable of controlling her own emotions. No tear would shame her cheek. It would not happen!

Yet Bird Shadow could never remember so much wanting to cry. She refused the urge, even though nobody would see. She would know. It was not seemly. To wail loudly and cry in a time of mourning was customary. It was not such a time. To cry because her man rode off on man's business was unthinkable.

She watched Fallon ride away. He was magnificent astride that chestnut gelding, she thought. She stared, unblinking, as the distance widened between them. She fought down her panic as he rode further and further away. She watched as his form dwindled in size. She squinted as summer haze made his image shimmer. She continued to stare after him when he topped a rise and dropped out of sight.

If she had heard herself sigh dejectedly, then again, then yet again, she would have blushed in shame. She was unaware she had done so. She was aware only of a great yawning gulf within her breast. It ached, deep inside, as it had one time when she had eaten spoiled liver. But this ache was worse. This ache was hollow and bottomless. It echoed in some hidden chamber of unspeakable emptiness.

She tore her eyes from the empty horizon and strode into the house. She removed her clothes. All these white-woman clothes. All these clothes that were part of a life she couldn't live without Fallon. All these clothes that made her weak and silly. It was fine, lacy under-clothes that made her soft and teary-eyed like white women.

She donned a set of the buckskins she had not worn for more than a month. She reveled in the strength of the leather. The cling of the strong hide to her legs reassured her. She almost giggled as she laced them, noticing they were tighter than she remembered.

Maybe she was gaining weight! Maybe she would yet gain the figure of the women of her race. She had plied Fallon with questions incessantly during the first months of their relationship.

'Are you not ashamed that your woman has no round stomach?'

'Do you envy men with fat wives to keep them warm in winter?'

'Do you wish I were even just a little fatter?'

'Are you sad my hips are not wider, like other women?'

Even though he always reassured her that she was beautiful in his eyes, she was never sure he was honest. She ate constantly to try to make her stomach rounder, her legs fatter, her face fuller, but to no avail.

She started to walk out the door, then stopped. She stared thoughtfully into space for fully five minutes.

Then she turned and took her Colt forty-five and holster from its peg beside the door. She belted it on, relishing the reassuring familiar weight of its presence. She checked its loads. She peered down its barrel. She practiced drawing it several times.

It was better. She felt less that cavern of emptiness now. It was there, a gnawing presence deep inside, but it was bearable. She was Bird Shadow. She was strong. She would make Fallon proud of how she took care of their home while he was gone.

The word 'gone' echoed in her mind, threatening a resurgence of the aching void within. Her jaw clamped. Her lips compressed to a thin line. She strode out of the house and went to see how the carpenters were progressing on the bunkhouse.

She visited with the carpenters' wives, as they prepared their husbands' dinners.

She declined the invitation to eat with them.

In the corral she roped a horse that she was training, and took him for a long ride. When she surrendered to her weariness, she retreated to the house. She slept on the floor in her buckskins. The bed was too unbearably empty.

A week crept agonizingly by. She shot a deer and dressed it out. Then she shared the meat with the carpenters. She took a haunch of it to both the Cranstons and the Hostlers. She staked out and scraped the hide carefully, then tanned it.

Ralph and Martha Cranston came and spent the better part of one day. They urged her to come visit them for a few days while Fallon was gone. She assured them she was deeply enjoying the freedom to do as she

94

pleased in his absence.

Virginia and Constance Hostler came another day. Virginia brought a basket of supplies and taught Bird Shadow the rudiments of quilting. The fabric was so much easier to sew than hides and leather, and the steel needles so much sharper, Bird Shadow was sewing like an old pro by the end of the day.

Three more days dragged past in sluggish reluctance.

The fourth day she heard horses approaching. They came from the opposite side of the house from the bunkhouse, where the carpenters were working. Inexplicable alarm bells sounded in her mind.

She checked her pistol and dropped it back in its holster. As she started outside she eyed the rifle in its rack, just at the side of the door. Without arguing with her intuition, she lifted it from the rack, checked its load, and tucked it under her arm.

Ranged before the door were four horsemen. She recognized Luther Grimes from the visit he and his wife had made their first week there. She guessed the young man who so resembled Luther's harsh scowl to be his son. From Fallon's description, she guessed the third man to be Stick Henderson. That meant the fourth was probably Fred Plymouth.

At a loss for words, she stared back into the palpable hatred of four sets of eyes. Luther Grimes broke the silence.

'You don't take advice too good, do you, Injun?'

As she focused on him, she vaguely noticed Stick Henderson begin easing his horse sideways, out of her field of vision. Fred Plymouth's loud voice forced her attention back.

'Where's that squaw man o' yours? Heard he rode out a few days ago. Did he go tepee creepin' to find hisself an extra squaw?'

The Grimes father and son duo guffawed loudly. Bird Shadow felt the blood rush to her face.

She shifted the rifle in the crook of her arm.

'It is my desire that you all leave,' she said, trying to keep the emotion from her voice.

The trio laughed together derisively.

'Now listen to that, would you!' said Fred Plymouth. 'Here's a two-bit squaw tryin' her best to sound like some high-falutin hussy! Are you going to make us leave, squaw?'

Bird Shadow's eyes narrowed. Fear and anger competed within her. She moved the rifle in her arm, grasping the forestock with her left hand, sliding her right hand back to the pistol grip. Her finger moved into the trigger guard. Deep fury quivered in her voice as she responded.

'I have asked you nicely. Now I am telling you. Get off my land!'

Fred Plymouth replied without losing his wide grin.

'Now that's what I like, boys. A woman with some fire. It's gonna be downright fun tamin' this two-bit squaw. We gonna draw straws to see who gets to mount 'er first?'

Bird Shadow lifted the barrel of the rifle to center on Plymouth's chest.

'If you think you are man enough to try that, take one step toward me. I have no compunctions against killing you.'

'You can't shoot fast enough to kill us all, even if you could hit us,' Luther interjected. 'We're gonna hold you down and let you find out what havin' some real white men is like. Then we're gonna run you plumb outa the country.'

'You shoulda left when Pa told you to,' young Garrison Grimes grinned. 'O' course, then we'da missed out on all the fun. I always wondered what a Injun woman'd be like.'

Out of the line of Bird Shadow's sight, Stick Henderson had kept his horse sidling away on an angle. When he was well behind her, while she was reacting to the overt and increasingly obscene threats of the other three, he quietly dismounted. He unfastened the strap holding his lariat onto the saddle. He stepped away from his horse, to a position directly behind Bird Shadow. He shook out a loop and began to whirl it slowly around his head.

His intention was clear. By dropping a loop over Bird Shadow's head, he could quickly pinion her arms to her body, rendering her incapable of either firing the rifle or drawing her pistol. That the four would then carry out their intentions with her was a foregone conclusion.

The circle of the loop Stick whirled widened. He braced to cast his loop. The three men, who could clearly see his actions, grinned in anticipation.

'I wouldn't do that!'

The words cut like an ice-cold knife through the heat of the moment. Henderson froze in mid-whirl of his lariat. The loop dropped to the ground.

The eyes of the other three men widened, then narrowed in anger and frustration.

'You best back up against the house, Bird Shadow,' the voice instructed. 'You let one o' them sneakin' coyotes get behind you.'

Aware for the first time that one of her assailants was unaccounted for in her vision, Bird Shadow fought for control. She backed swiftly toward the house until she felt its wall behind her, keeping her rifle barrel centered on Fred Plymouth.

As she did, the scene behind her came into view. Stick Henderson still stood like a statue, holding the loop that now trailed behind him on the ground. Behind him, Ralph Cranston stood with a rifle pointed squarely at the cowboy's back.

Henderson, reading the faces of his friends, understood his peril. The pasty pallor of his skin left no doubt of his fear.

'What're you doin' here, Cranston?' Plymouth demanded.

'Just checkin' on a neighbor,' Ralph responded. 'The better question is what are you boys doin' here? You didn't happen to plan somethin' that'd get all four of you hanged, did you?'

The younger Grimes's face lost its color abruptly. His father was less affected, but clearly disturbed by the words.

'There ain't no law in this country protectin' squaws,' Plymouth insisted.

'As a matter of fact, there is,' Ralph corrected. 'You're already trespassing with evil intent. The lady can shoot you all like the dogs you are, and the law wouldn't touch her. Beyond that, you clearly stated your intention to commit rape. That not only gives her husband the legal right to hunt you all down and kill you, it gives the law the right to hang you. Rape is a hanging offense, you know.'

'Not when it's just some squaw!' Plymouth insisted.

'Even if she were "just some squaw", it does,' Ralph argued. 'But the lady isn't just some squaw. She happens to be the wife of a friend of mine. Now you boys best ride outa here before I change my mind about lettin' you. And if you set foot on this lady's property again, or if I hear one of you, or even hear about one of you, saying anything I think demeans her character, either I or Fallon will be comin' after you. Do you understand that?'

Both of the Grimeses nodded their heads vigorously. Stick coiled his rope and mounted his horse, moving as if to leave the yard. Only Plymouth remained defiant.

'You'll be sorry you butted into something that ain't none o' your business,' he blustered. 'You ain't heard the last o' this. You'll be run outa the country just like her when word gets around you're hanging around here cozy with a squaw while her ol' man's outa the country. Squaw-lovers ain't too popular 'round here.'

Blood rushed to Ralph's face, then ebbed away leaving a white fury behind.

'You wanta get off that horse and say that, Plymouth? Right now! Either shut your foul mouth and get outa here or step off that horse. If you don't do one or the other, so help me I'll shoot you off of it.'

Only a little of the bluster left Plymouth. He reined his horse around to leave the yard, but he shot over his shoulder:

'You best not show your face in town, Cranston! I'm tellin' ya!'

He kicked his horse into a gallop. The others followed, leaving the yard in a cloud of dust.

As Bird Shadow lowered her rifle and sagged back against the house for support, the carpenters came running from the bunkhouse.

'What's going on?' Virgil called out. 'Is there any trouble?'

'Not now,' Ralph assured them. 'But there was.'

'What happened?'

'Fred Plymouth, Stick Henderson, along with Luther and Gar Grimes thought they'd catch Bird Shadow alone. They rode up on the far side of the house so you boys wouldn't see 'em. I 'spect they intended to stick somethin' in her mouth so she couldn't yell loud enough for you to hear.'

The two carpenters gaped, wordless for several heart-beats.

'They were gonna ... They was ... Over my dead body they were! You want us to saddle up and we'll ride after 'em?'

Ralph shook his head.

'No. Just leave it. Fallon'll take care of it, I have an idea.'

Even so, the carpenters promised that one of their wives would be inseparable from Bird Shadow until Fallon returned.

100

CHAPTER 12

Greater thunder in her heart than a herd of buffalo. Greater joy than she could remember. Greater relief than she would ever admit.

A herd of 200 head of cattle was no tidal wave of beef, but it was wonderful! It was their herd! More important, it was her husband returning!

When she first heard the distant yipping of the drovers and bawling of the cows, Bird Shadow raced to the barn. She saddled her horse with hands that trembled in spite of her best efforts, leaped astride her bay mare and raced from the yard to meet her returning man.

She spotted him at once, red beard shining in the Wyoming sun, tall in the saddle, buckskins setting him apart from the cowhands.

As she approached, she forced her horse to slow. By the time they met, her lifetime of conditioning to maintain 'her place', her ingrained reticence at publicly embarrassing her husband with any display of affection, had reasserted itself. She held her horse to a trot and rode to him. She reined in her horse so they sat facing each other, side by side.

Fallon had no such reticence. All he said was: 'Aaaah!'

He reached out a muscular arm and swept her from the saddle, lifting her to his own. A small squeak of surprise escaped her lips at the unexpected action. She came to rest on the front of his saddle, between him and the saddle horn, facing sideways. He wrapped both arms around her, smothering her mouth with his own, erasing more than two weeks of loneliness with the taste of her lips.

Her hunger for him was no less than his for her. She forgot all inhibitions, responding with total abandon to his caress. All the world faded to insignificance. The herd of cattle was no longer there. Her fear and shame and anger disappeared. There was nothing at all in her universe except her man, his arms around her, his lips conveying so eloquently how much he had missed her.

She wanted that moment to last for ever, but such moments are not meant to do so. She leaned away from him and brushed a hand across his matted beard.

'You need a bath, my husband,' she said.

He roared with laughter.

'Two weeks gone and all I get is told I need a bath? What kind of welcome is that, woman?'

Her eyes danced and shone.

'You will learn that after you take that bath, smelly old man!'

He erupted with laughter again.

'Well, ain't you the saucy one! To tell the truth, that bath sounds almost as good as the hints about what follows it.'

'Did everything go well?' she changed the subject,

102

suddenly uncomfortable with such personal conversation with the drovers in clear sight. Her presence, sitting in his saddle, seemed suddenly too close, too constricted, too demonstrative. She grasped the saddle horn with one hand, laid the other on his thigh, and boosted herself clear of his saddle, sliding to the ground to land lightly on her feet.

She walked quickly to where her horse waited, reins trailing on the ground. She stepped into the saddle and turned back to her husband. She again rode up beside him, facing him, but with enough distance to keep him from sweeping her from the saddle again. She studied his face, waiting for his response to her question.

Half a dozen emotions flitted across his face, mostly hidden beneath the red screen of his beard.

'Mostly. No real big trouble,' he said, his voice betraying cautios restraint.

'You had trouble?' she probed.

'A mite. No more than what you'd expect. We run into a bunch o' Pawnee.'

Her eyes betrayed her surprise.

'Pawnee? So far west?'

He nodded. 'Game's scarce in their country. Been a drouth, sounds like. They were a pretty hungry lot.'

'How many were there?'

'Upwards of twenty-five.'

'Did you have to fight?'

He shook his head. 'Naw. I sorta felt sorry for 'em. We'd lost three calves, so I had three cows without none. I gave 'em the three cows.'

She considered it silently for a moment.

'It is better to give three cows than have to fight. I

would have deep sorrow if a Pawnee wounded my husband.'

He nodded. 'They were desperate enough to've taken us on, no doubt. I kinda felt bad just giving them three.'

'Was there no more trouble?'

'We did have a brush with some rustlers tryin' to steal a bunch o' cows. We shot all but one. We hung the other one.'

Silence hung between them for several seconds as the implications paraded through each of their minds. Fallon broke the silence.

'Did it go well with you?'

An instant's hesitation flickered in her eyes, and was instantly blanked out by a bland and expressionless return of his gaze.

'Yes. But I was lonely without my husband. I did not sleep in our bed while you were gone.'

'What? You didn't? Where'd you sleep?'

'I slept on the floor. The bed was too empty. Now it will be good again.'

Nothing more was said about that time until Ralph and Martha Cranston came to call several days later. Even then it was a chance remark during the noon meal.

In response to a casual mention of how good it was for the carpenters that their wives could be there with them instead of home alone, Martha observed: 'I'm sure glad Ralph decided to ride up and check on Bird Shadow that day.'

Bird Shadow's head jerked up, staring first at Martha, then at her husband. Fallon stopped in mid-bite. His frown drew his red hair down until it threatened to meet his beard.

'Did something happen you didn't tell me about, Bird Shadow?'

Martha's hand flew to her mouth, aware too late she had spoken out of turn.

Ralph concentrated intently on his food, stealing furtive glances toward Bird Shadow from beneath his brows.

Silence hung in the room. It seemed to drip from the ceiling beams and seep through the pores of their skin. Bird Shadow's eyes slowly rose to meet her husband's.

'I did not think it anything worth troubling my husband,' she said softly.

Fallon laid his fork on the table. His voice, just as soft, was nonetheless edged with steel.

'Well, maybe you'd best let me decide that. What happened?'

She shrugged, dropping her eyes back to her plate.

'It was only some men who wanted not to have an Indian living in the valley.'

Fallon glared at his wife for a long moment, then swivelled his eyes to his friend.

'Ralph, maybe you'd be easier to pry it out of. What happened?'

Ralph cleared his throat uneasily. He shifted in his seat. He glanced at his wife, then at Bird Shadow, then met Fallon's gaze.

'I 'spect she'da handled it without no help from me,' he observed.

'Handle what?'

Ralph took a deep breath.

'Four o' the scum o' the valley found out you was outa the country. They rode up, plannin' to . . . abuse Bird Shadow an' run 'er outa the country. They slipped up on the off side o' the house, so the carpenters didn't spot 'em. Bird Shadow met 'em with a rifle, but one of 'em slipped around behind 'er. He was fixin' ta dab a rope on 'er, when I dealt myself in. I'd rode up jist ta check on 'er. I throwed a polecat inta their plans. They rode off, but they been threatenin' ta abuse Bird Shadow's an' my reputation some.'

Fallon's face was nearly as red as his bristling beard. 'Who was it?' he growled.

Ralph glanced at Bird Shadow again before he answered, offering her the opportunity to disclose the names. When she silently demurred, he said:

'Fred Plymouth, Stick Henderson, Luther Grimes an' his kid, Gar.'

Fallon shot a burning gaze around the table, then rose wordlessly. He disappeared into the bedroom. Silence resumed its grip on the trio left at the table.

In minutes, Fallon reappeared. He once again wore the familiar buckskins. His shorter-barreled forty-five Colt was in his right holster. The longer-barreled version of the same gun was in his left holster, butt forward. The big knife was in its customary place just behind the left gun.

'I 'spect I'll take a little ride to town.'

'I'll go with you,' Ralph asserted at once.

Martha's words were torn from her before she even paused to think.

'Ralph! You promised!'

Ralph stood up from the table. Martha's words

stopped Fallon in his tracks. He looked back and forth between Ralph and Martha, trying to fathom the meaning of the words.

Ralph threw a look of apology to his wife.

'Fallon, I hung up my guns when we come to this valley,' he said. 'We both aimed to start a new life. You folks has been friends, an' you'd jist as well know. Afore me'n Martha met, I made a livin' with my gun. If folks knowed my real name, they'd be lawmen from half a dozen places scroungin' around the valley tryin' to collect a reward.'

Fallon studied his friend for a long moment.

'You coverin' my back?'

'You're covered. We'll stop by my place for my guns.'

Fallon nodded once and strode toward the door. Ralph carefully avoided the frantic but burning glare from his wife as he followed.

CHAPTER 13

Fallon and Ralph reined up before One Eyed Jack's saloon. They each looked carefully up and down the street before dismounting.

'They're here,' Fallon said. Ralph nodded. 'Recognized the brands on the horses.'

'It's my party,' Fallon insisted.

Ralph nodded. 'I got your back. The rest o' the party's all yours.'

They stepped through the door of the saloon swiftly, each taking a step to opposite sides, then waiting for their eyes to adjust.

A long bar ran the length of the room, at a right angle to the front wall, three steps to the left of the door. Tables were scattered around the rest of the floor. A piano stood beside a small stage at the back wall. A door in the rear opened onto a hallway that afforded doors into several small rooms.

The four men they sought sat at a table near the piano. A half-empty bottle of whiskey sat on the table. They, along with one man Fallon didn't know, were involved in a game of cards.

Stick Henderson looked up as Fallon and Ralph

entered. He spotted Fallon, but appeared not to see Ralph. He said something Fallon could not hear. The other heads all jerked up at his words, shocked by Fallon's sudden appearance.

Fallon's voice broke like a rifle shot across the room.

'Plymouth! You and these three pieces of bog slime you're sitting with came to my house while I was gone to try to rape my wife!'

All noise stopped. The bartender froze in place, a tilted bottle ready to refill a glass that waited in vain for a drop of the liquor to fall. Every eye in the saloon darted back and forth between Fallon and Plymouth.

Plymouth turned beet-red. His eyes flashed around the room. He looked at his companions, visibly weighing their advantage in numbers. The count restored his courage, aiding him past the first seconds of panic. His voice was taunting.

'Well, well! If it ain't the squaw man! We heard you went up north to add another Injun whore to your collection. Did you find one?'

Fallon crossed the floor, stopping scarcely three feet in front of the leering homesteader. In the deathly silence Fallon's words were as brittle as glass.

'Plymouth, you're as rotten a low-down lying excuse for a yellow-bellied coward that ever walked the earth. I aim to beat you within an inch of your life or else shoot you where you sit. Which'll it be?'

Plymouth's eyes darted to his companions. Each of them visibly pulled back away from him. Gar Grimes left his chair and backed against the wall. The others, as unobtrusively as possible, began to slide their chairs, isolating Plymouth.

He was a loudmouth, but he wasn't stupid. He thought he had a chance against Fallon in a brawl. He knew he didn't with a gun. He lunged from the chair, trying to catch Fallon by surprise with a shoulder in the stomach.

Fallon was far too quick. He sidestepped, chopping a hard right into the side of the stout homesteader's head as he lunged past. It staggered him, but he regained his balance and righted himself. He whirled, directly into the path of a straight left that smacked into his face with the sound of a water-melon being struck with a fence post. Blood flew in all directions.

A right hook came immediately behind the left, and the bones of Fred's jaw crunched audibly. A left into his wind doubled him over, but a swift right uppercut straightened him again.

Fallon stepped in close, hammering ribs with a left, then a right, then a left, then a right, working method-ically up the rib cage. Every time a fist struck, another rib fractured. With each blow, Fred reeled a step back-ward, fighting to keep his feet. Just before he could gather his balance another blow would fall, driving him back another step.

Then the back wall of the saloon prevented any further retreat. Standing him erect with another sharp uppercut, Fallon lifted a knee into Fred's groin. The force of the blow lifted his feet easily six inches from the floor.

He doubled over in a paroxysm of pain he was no longer conscious enough to feel. He didn't even feel the same knee crush his face, driving all his front teeth from their sockets, as Fallon's hands behind his head

110

added force to the effect of the upward directed blow of the knee.

Without looking at the prostrate homesteader, Fallon whirled just in time to dodge a chair aimed at the back of his head by Stick Henderson. As he stepped aside he lashed out with a foot, catching Stick's knee from the side just as his whole weight rocked forward onto that foot. He screamed in pain and started to fall sideways.

Whirling, Fallon drove his right instep into Stick's side just below the ribs, driving him back upright. He stepped around in front of the breathless Henderson and sent a left jab toward his face.

Somehow the rangy homesteader managed to dodge the jab. It passed just beside his face, barely grazing the skin.

Instead of withdrawing the fist Fallon stepped forward. Letting his fist pass on beyond Stick's face, he wrapped his arm around the tall man's neck, jerking his head forward and down, held like a vise in a headlock. Using his weight and uncanny strength, Fallon pushed down on the back of the man's neck while he tilted his face upward to meet the oncoming right fist. Fallon's right fist began a rhythmic piston action, pounding relentlessly into the face of the helpless victim.

Fallon wasn't even aware of when Stick lost consciousness. The red tide of his rage vented in the pounding of his fist into an increasingly formless and bloody mass that had once been a face.

At last Fallon realized that the man was hanging limply in the grip of his arm, totally unconscious.

He dropped him and turned toward the Grimes duo

of father and son. Both men were now standing against the back wall of the saloon. Each had his hands outstretched in front of him. It was the elder Grimes who spoke.

'My son was jist along 'cause I tol' 'im to, Fallon. He don't deserve no beatin'. I do, an' ya kin beat me ta death, I 'spect. I won't blame ya none. That was the rottenest thing I ever let anyone talk me inta, ridin' up there like that. But we wasn't aimin' ta do nothin' ta your missus. Honest we wasn't. Well, me'n Garrison didn't. I'd like ta think we wouldn'ta stood fer Fred er Stick doin' nothin' like they said, neither. But they said it, an' we didn't say nothin' ta stop 'em. But ya gotta know afore ya beat me er kill me, that I am sure sorry. I'm sorry I let Fred talk us inta goin'. I'm sorry I didn't say nothin' when Fred started spreadin' them rumors an' such. I'm . . . well, I'm sorry. Thet's all. Now you do what ya gotta do.'

Fallon had stopped half-way to the duo when Luther began to speak. He stayed there, fighting the fury that had robbed him of reason. He glared first at Luther, then at Garrison. Something in their gaze penetrated the mindless fires of his wrath.

He took a deep breath. He looked down at his fists, red with blood. He brushed at the blood that spattered and smeared odd patterns across his buckskins. He looked at the pair again. His voice was soft, but hard as granite.

'If you ever say a word about my wife, or even look cross-eyed at her, I'll kill you both.'

He wheeled and walked toward the door.

His anger had been too focused. His rage had been

112

too directed, too blind, too unthinking. He had noticed, then totally ignored the fifth man at that table. It was a mistake that had taken the lives of better men than Kerwin O'Fallon.

That other man had stood and stepped clear of the table when the fracas first began. He stood with his hand on his gun, never moving, watching the action with obvious relish. When Fallon turned his back and walked toward the door, he made his move.

Swiftly and silently his hand arced up from his holster gripping a Russian forty-four. Even if he had seen it, Fallon could never have turned and drawn his own weapon in time.

Fallon wasn't the only one guilty of a lapse of observation. The gunman had failed to notice Ralph, standing still, just beside the door he and Fallon had entered together.

With blurring speed Ralph's own hand swept up, Colt forty-five in his grip, even as he shouted:

'Look out behind ya!' at Fallon.

Before Fallon could even react Ralph's gun barked three times, so closely spaced it sounded as one extended roar. The gunman's Russian forty-four answered, but its barrel was already sagging toward the floor. Its bullet harmlessly penetrated the floor. The gunman dropped to his knees. Fallon turned just in time to note three closely spaced holes in the man's shirt, just over the heart, before he fell forward into the sawdust.

'Anybody else wanta buy in?' Ralph's soft voice asked quietly.

Nobody in the room dared even to breathe, lest the

breath be heard as a challenge. Then Marshal Walker burst through the door, a sawed-off double-barreled shotgun in his hands.

'What's going on in here?'

Nobody moved as the marshal stood, letting his eyes adjust. His gaze shot around the room. It took in the crumpled forms of Fred Plymouth and Stick Henderson, unrecognizable and covered with blood. He assessed the obviously dead form of the gunman. His eyes scanned across Ralph, whose gun still covered the room, standing as if carved from marble. They came to rest on Fallon. He looked him up and down, noting the copious amounts of blood that smeared his buckskins and splattered his face.

'You best explain what's goin' on here, Fallon,' he ordered in a no-nonsense tone.

Fallon nodded. He took a deep breath and let it out slowly, shaping the words in his mind. Hal Walker waited, his shotgun still held at the ready.

'I rode off for a couple weeks,' Fallon said. 'Went over toward Cheyenne and bought us a herd of them red white-faces. Drove 'em home. While I was gone, Fred Plymouth, Stick Henderson, Luther Grimes and his son Gar rode out to my place. They ordered my wife out of the valley, then tried to rope her. They told her they were going to take turns on her before they ran her out of the valley. They'd have done it if Ralph hadn't ridden over to my place to check on her. He let 'em ride off. When I found out about it, I came to town looking for them. I found them.'

Walker's eyes darted around the room again, settling on Luther Grimes.

'Is that true, Luther?'

Luther nodded solemnly. He cleared his throat.

'It's true, Marshal. Every word of it. Then Fred, he started spreadin' it around thet Ralph was layin' up with the . . . with Fallon's wife, while Fallon was gone. Me'n Gar deserved to get beat too, truth be told.'

Walker's eyes made another tour of the room.

'Who's that one?' he indicated the motionless form on the floor.

Nobody spoke. He turned to Ralph.

'I'm askin' you, Cranston. Who's he?'

Ralph shook his head, but nothing else on his body moved.

'I ain't got no idee, Marshal. He was sittin' with them four when we come in. I promised Fallon I'd jist cover 'is back. When he turned his back to leave, that feller drew on 'im, to shoot 'im in the back. He wasn't quick enough.'

Walker turned his attention back to Grimes.

'Who is he, Luther?'

Luther shrugged. 'Don't rightly know much about him. Said his name's Wes Black. He was some friend o' Fred's. Jist drifted in a week er so ago.'

Once more Walker surveyed the room, then he lowered his shotgun. He spoke to the bartender.

'Oscar, you best have somebody carry those two over to Doc's. Get the undertaker for the gunman. Tell 'im the town'll pay for the buryin'. Somebody best go tell Prudence her man's in bad shape.'

He turned his attention to Fallon. 'That ain't the way to make friends, Fallon.'

'At least it cuts down some on enemies,' Fallon answered.

At a loss for an answer, the marshal turned and walked out of the saloon, followed by Fallon and Ralph.

CHAPTER 14

'It seemed odd, even to Bird Shadow,' Fallon asserted.

Both Ralph and Martha Cranston turned their eyes to Bird Shadow. She stared thoughtfully, her eyes distant.

'If she had been an Indian girl, it wouldn't have been so strange,' she said. 'It was odd, though, for a white woman to say nothing at all.'

'Introduced her as his wife, though, huh?'

Fallon nodded. 'They came in the mercantile store while we were there. We'd just accepted Jane's invitation to supper. You know how Jane is. This couple she didn't know came in, and she was "Oh my goodness," all over them.'

The other three laughed appreciatively. 'She sure doesn't let anyone stay a stranger very long,' Ralph agreed.

'She was my first friend in Boxelder,' Bird Shadow chimed in. 'It was so nice to find someone friendly the first place we stopped. I don't think I could have dealt with all the . . . animosity? Is that the word? I couldn't have dealt with all the animosity from other people if it wasn't for meeting Jane first, then Ellen, then the other women in town. They were so nice.'

'Oh, by the way, did you hear about Henderson?' Ralph changed the subject.

Fallon nodded. 'Heard when we were in town. I didn't realize I'd killed him. I guess I was madder'n I thought I was.'

'You were a wild man,' Ralph agreed. 'But Plymouth survived.'

'But he's still in pretty bad shape,' Martha added. 'It serves him right. I'm sorry you didn't kill him too.'

'They left last week,' Ralph added.

Fallon nodded. 'Just as well. I heard Prudence asked the neighbors to help 'er load up all their stuff in their wagon, as soon as Fred could travel. Made him a bed in the wagon, 'cause he can't sit up yet.'

Ralph shook his head. 'That has to be plumb painful, bouncin' along in a wagon with that many busted ribs.'

'Can't be more than he had coming.'

'I can't argue with that. Prudence told Esther Wilson they were going to find some place to settle that didn't have all the "Indian lovers".'

'Maybe we'll be lucky and they'll run into them Pawnee,' Fallon observed.

Martha brought the conversation back to the subject from which it had strayed. 'So what about the new couple? Do they have a homestead?'

'Yup. They're your new neighbors,' Fallon offered. 'Their place is about half-way between yours and town. They homesteaded that quarter just above the beaver dam.'

'I've wondered why nobody'd filed on that,' Ralph remarked. 'It's a nice spot.'

'What are their names?' Martha persisted.

'Jim and Wilma Turner,' Fallon replied.

Martha gasped. Three sets of eyes whipped to her face. Her sudden pallor was stark and unexpected.

'You know that name?' Fallon asked.

'Tell me what he looked like,' Martha insisted instead of answering.

'Well, he's a big man,' Fallon described. 'In fact, he introduced himself as Big Jim. He's all of six feet four or five. Stout fellow. An ax-handle across the shoulders. Smiles easy. Talk your leg off.'

'But his wife looks afraid to say a word,' Bird Shadow interrupted. 'Even when Jane asked her a question, her husband would answer for her.'

'And she'd just look at the floor, every time,' Fallon added.

'Did he have a scar?' Martha insisted.

Fallon looked at Martha, then Ralph, before he answered.

'Well, as a matter of fact, he does. Big scar on his face, along his left jaw. The whole length of his jaw. What it put me in mind of, is someone tried to cut his throat and got too high.'

Martha's pallor deepened. Her jaw clamped until the muscles at the hinge of her jaw bulged. Her eyes clouded over, becoming distant, but some deep fire burned within them.

Ralph was studying her face intently.

'Is that him?' he asked softly.

'That's him,' Martha said just as softly. 'It couldn't be anyone else.'

Fallon and Bird Shadow looked at each other in

confusion, then back at Martha.

'Somebody you know, I take it,' Fallon observed.

Instead of responding, Martha looked at her husband.

'Can I tell them?' Ralph studied her face a moment longer, then shrugged her shoulders.

'If you want to. It's your decision. They already know a lot about us. If we're gonna be friends, they'd just as well know it all.'

Attention shifted back to Martha. She looked at Bird Shadow.

'You already know part of it, Bird Shadow.'

Fallon's eyebrows lifted. He had never known his wife to keep anything from him. That she knew some secret of Martha's and kept it from him came as a surprise. He said nothing, content to wait.

Martha took a deep breath and began, speaking rapidly.

'When I was twelve, my father was killed. About a year later, my mother married Jim Turner. He was really nice at first, but he kept getting more and more . . . he started hugging me a lot, and brushing his hands over me. Then one day when my mother was gone, he raped me. He told me if I told my mother, or anyone, he would kill us both. I believed him. After that, he found all kinds of ways to get me alone so he could do it again. He made me do all kinds of disgusting things with him.'

Her determination lost its momentum and she lapsed into silence. A shudder ran through her, as she let her memory deal with things long suppressed. Ralph reached out a hand and took hers.

The touch of her husband's hand visibly strengthened her, and she continued.

'When I got a chance, I ran away. By then Jim and mother had taken in another girl. A twelve-year-old. Her parents were both killed in a buggy wreck. I didn't want to run away, because I knew Jim would abuse her instead of me, but in the end I couldn't take it any more. I left right after he went to town one day, when I could get a head start.'

'Did he ever come looking for you?' Fallon asked. She shook her head.

'I don't know. I went several places and tried to find a job. I found one job as a domestic helper, but I wasn't there a month before the husband made it clear he expected the same things Jim did. To make a long story short, I ended up doing the only thing I knew how to do to survive. I became a whore.'

Fallon tried hard not to register any surprise. From Bird Shadow's expression, he knew the revelation came as no surprise to her. They all waited in silence for Martha to continue. It was Ralph who took up the story.

'She jist started workin' at the Six Mile Hog Ranch. I'd been shot up some, an' made it there to hole up. She took me in an' nursed me. Saved my life. I promised her when I got well I'd take her outa there, we'd both change our names, and we'd start over together.'

'So you came here and homesteaded,' Fallon conjectured.

Ralph nodded. Martha merely stared at the table. Fallon said softly:

'Now the past has caught up with you.'

Bitterness gave Martha's words a hard, brittle edge.

'So it would seem.'

'I seen you draw on that guy in One Eyed Jack's,' Fallon said. 'I knew you had to be a gunman. I'm faster'n greased lightning with a gun, but I couldn't hold a candle to you.' He turned his attention back to Martha. 'Do you think he'd know you now?'

Martha shook her head.

'It's been nine years. I've changed. A lot. But I'd know him. I can guarantee that.'

'So you think this Turner's wife is the kid they took in?'

'I'd bet my life on it,' Martha concurred.

'Then what happened to your ma?'

There was a long pause before Martha answered.

'I don't know. I never tried to get in touch with her because I knew Jim would intercept any message I could send. But I know people there. I'm not afraid any more. We'll go to town tomorrow, and I'll send some telegrams.'

The air grew suddenly heavy with portent of days to come.

CHAPTER 15

Fallon stepped from the barn at the sound of a running horse approaching. He brushed a hand over the gun butt at his hip, then lifted it and dropped it back into the holster, making sure it was loose and free.

He watched the dust cloud approach. Bird Shadow walked across the yard swiftly to stand at his side. Before Fallon could make out the identity of the approaching rider, Bird Shadow spoke.

'It is Robert Hostler.'

Fallon nodded and walked out into the yard to meet the onrushing neighbor. Bird Shadow moved soundlessly at his side.

Robert skidded his horse to a stop before them.

'They's been a killin', Fallon! All hell's gonna bust loose.'

Fallon's face remained as inscrutable as his wife's.

'Who got killed?'

'You know the Richmans?'

'Sure. They got the homestead clear out at the end of the valley.'

Robert nodded. 'You know their kid? Shane?'

'We know them.'

'That's the ones.'

'The ones that got killed?'

'Yup.'

'Will and Shane both?'

'Yup.'

'Who killed them? How?'

'Shot 'em. Dang kid never had a chance. Well, neither one of 'em did.'

'Who shot them?'

'Hargess and Winkler.'

'I don't know anybody by either name.'

'They're two o' them new hands the Fanchers hired.'

Fallon mulled the information.

'Well, you best get down and let me rub that horse down, and you can tell us what's going on.'

Robert dismounted and Fallon took the reins, leading the sweat-soaked horse into the barn. He began to rub him down with a burlap bag as Robert began to talk.

'You knew Fanchers've swore they'd run us all outa this valley, didn't ya?'

Fallon nodded without answering.

'You knowed how they've been crowdin' cows in on us, didn't ya?'

'They've been doing that for two or three months. They used to graze this valley in the summer, and clear up into the mountains behind my place. I guess it stands to reason they'd be upset, having the whole valley homesteaded like it is. They've offered to buy everybody out, at one time or another. Us included. They've blustered and threatened, but I didn't think they'd do much more than that.'

124

'Well, they been doin' more'n that. They beat up a couple o' guys purty bad. Not as bad as you did Fred 'n Stick, but plenty bad. They drove bunches o' cows through several people's fields an' ruined the crops. They dropped a dead coyote down Wilson's well. Left 'em without water fer a month, an' them with baby Faith ta take keer of. Her'n the baby went over an' stayed with her folks, till Luther an' Ev got the well cleaned out an' all. Over the past month they've tried ta bait half a dozen guys inta drawin' on 'em, but nobody'd take the bait. Not till Will 'n Shane. All the time, they keep pushin' more an' more cattle up the valley.'

Robert stopped suddenly, as if all the air had gone out of him, leaving a despondent and frustrated shell. Fallon nodded again.

'I knew part of it. I didn't know it was getting that bad. They even had their hands push one bunch of Rafter J cattle all the way up here. We didn't realize it until a day or two later, but we didn't think a lot about it. We just herded them back onto Rafter J land.'

Robert nodded. 'Thet's what everyone else's been doin', too. Only yesterday Will Richman and two of his kids, Shane an' Beulah, I think the girl's name is. Anyway, them an' Carl Larson was pushin' a bunch o' Rafter J stock back onto their own range. Two o' them gunhands o' Fanchers' caught 'em doin' it. They had words. They threatened to kill 'em. Will lost his head an' went for his gun. He didn't even have it outa the holster afore Winkler put two bullets in 'im. Then Shane made a grab fer 'is dad's gun, an' Hargess shot him too.'

'Shot the kid?'

'Shot 'im right between the eyes. Laughed while he was doin' it. Then Winkler dropped a rope on Carl an' took off draggin' 'im with his horse.'

'He drug him?'

'He drug 'im around in a big circle till he was pertn-eart dead, and drug him back to where Beulah was bawlin' over her dad an' her brother. He told her to go tell the rest of us — sodbusters, he called us — that if we didn't either sell out to Fanchers er just up an' quit the country, they'd be killin' us all. Then they jist rode off an' left that pore little ol' girl there with two dead men an' one pertneart dead.'

Fallon busied himself with rubbing the horse down far more than was necessary. He digested the information carefully before he answered.

'So what is everyone planning to do?'

Robert's chin jutted forward.

'They been havin' meetin's all summer, tryin' ta figger out what ta do. They ain't included you 'n me 'n Ralph, on account o' some of 'em's still down on you an' Bird Shadow. Anyway, they was a big meetin' at Richman's place right after they buried Will an' Shane. It was split pertneart down the middle, between givin' up an' sellin' out to Fanchers, er fightin'. Then Dorothy Richman made a speech that shamed the britches off o' the ones that wanted to cut an' run. She said her an' Beulah was stayin', no matter what, and after her husband and her son had paid for that land with their blood, if anyone ran away they'd best not never look at themselves in a mirror again. She said if they did, all they'd see was yeller, every time they tried ta shave, fer the rest o' their lives. The Walton family packed up an' left anyway, but that's all.'

'They sent word to you?'

Robert nodded. 'They'd sent special word to me an' Ralph. That's why we was at the meetin'. We mentioned you was the best one in the valley to figger out what ta do. Even the ones that'd held out finally agreed, an' asked me if I'd come talk to ya.'

Fallon was lost in thought for a long while. His voice was soft, like hard steel wrapped in thin cloth, as he spoke to Bird Shadow.

'I'll saddle our horses, Bird Shadow. You fix us some food for a few days. Change your clothes.'

Without questioning, Bird Shadow turned and walked swiftly toward the house.

'What you gonna do?' Robert asked.

There was another long pause before Fallon asked:

'Is there another meeting?'

Robert nodded. 'There's one tonight. Back at Richman's. They 'specially want you an' me an' Ralph there. Word's got around thet Ralph's some kinda gunman, an' they know you're hell on high red wheels in a fight. They're purty much waitin' fer someone thet knows how to tell 'em how to fight a big outfit like Fanchers'.'

Fallon nodded. 'We don't have enough guns, or enough experienced fighters to meet them head on. They'll want us to, but it would be suicide. We'll have to make them come to us.'

'How can we do that?'

Fallon's eyes were distant for several minutes. A

gleam flickered in some deep pool within his icy-blue eyes.

'That's my department. Mine and Bird Shadow's. You tell the bunch of them to keep guards posted, but to not try to move any Rafter J cows, or anything that'll play into their hands. We'll be gone three days. Four days from now, at sunset, have everybody meet at Richman's.'

'What about Walker?'

'What about him?'

'Well, he's the marshal. Killin' Will an' Shane was murder. Ain't it his place to go arrest Hargess an' Winkler?'

Fallon shook his head.

'He's a town marshal, not a United States marshal. He doesn't have any legal jurisdiction outside of Boxelder. But he's a good man. After you give everyone else the message, you or Ralph can ride in and let him know what's going on. Tell him, if he wants to buy into the festivities he can be at that meeting. He's welcome to bring along as many men from town as he thinks would be good in a fight. The more guns we can enlist the better.'

Robert frowned at Fallon for several moments.

'I know you ain't gonna tell me what you're plannin' to do. Kin ya tell me what Fanchers is gonna do?'

Fallon nodded. 'They're going to bring their whole crew, fighting mad, all at once. From their perspective, they'll be coming to clean out the whole nest of sodbusters from the valley. They'll start at the lower end of the valley. Their plan will be to sweep up the whole valley, burn every building, kill all the stock, and kill any people who get in their way. And they won't come by daylight. They'll come by night. A week from tonight will be full moon. I'm banking on that being when they'll make their play.'

'You think it'll be a full-blown range war that way?'

'No question about it. Except we'll be ready, and they'll be rattled. Unless I miss my guess, they'll be short about half of their gun hands by then, too.'

Robert shook his head. 'Now you've really got me buffaloed.'

'There's a fresh horse in the end stall down there. You'd best ride him back. Yours is pretty well worn out. Give him enough feed and water and leave him in a stall. Then you can come back and trade horses with me tomorrow. Turn mine out in the pasture with a pair of hobbles.'

'I sure wish ya'd let me know what you're plannin'.'

Fallon ignored the request. 'My two hands, Russ and Joe, are about a mile up that left draw, checking out the cows that wandered over that way,' he said. 'Ride up there before you go back, and take them with you. Tell them to load for bear, and stay down there and help stand guard on the places at the end of the valley until I get back.'

'You ain't even gonna tell me where you're gonna git back from, are ya.'

'Just give everybody the message. A couple of 'em'll squawk some about taking orders from a squaw man, but don't let that rattle you. They'll figure out soon enough that none of them has a better idea.'

Robert nodded at that.

'They've already figured that out. That's why they

sent me to make sure you and Ralph are at this meeting.'

'Then you and Ralph will have to persuade them to trust me. Better yet, tell them Bird Shadow has a plan, and I said it would work.'

Sarcasm dripped from Robert's voice.

'Oh, that'll help persuade 'em!'

Fallon grinned. 'That's going to be half the fun. I'm already imagining what it'll be like to watch Luther Grimes thank Bird Shadow for saving his homestead.'

The grin was not contagious. Robert looked like he'd rather start at the wrong end and eat a raw skunk than deliver Fallon's message that way. On the other hand, he knew he'd better do as he was told, if he wanted Fallon to be his friend. He sure wanted that. Especially just now.

CHAPTER 16

The Indian village virtually ignored their entrance, to all appearances. It was neither the first nor the last time that appearance and reality diverged wildly.

Their approach had been reported an hour before. Fallon was unmistakable, even from a distance, with the bushy red beard that caught the sunlight.

From the first report word flew as if by magic. It spread outward like a drop of oil on water, until every member of the village was coated with it.

Yet when they entered the village there was nobody to greet them. They were neither challenged nor welcomed. They stopped, in accordance with custom, in the center of the village. They sat their horses, silently, waiting.

The wait was courteously brief. In little more than three minutes Striking Eagle stepped from his lodge, flanked by Hides From Bear and Blind Buffalo. Behind them four more Shoshone warriors ranged.

'Red Beard and his woman are welcome,' Striking Eagle announced. 'It has been a long time since you visited our village.'

'My friends and the people of my wife have never

been far from my mind,' Fallon replied in fluent Shoshone. 'It is good to come back to visit.'

Striking Eagle called a command over his shoulder. Two young boys came running to take the horses. Fallon and Bird Shadow dismounted, handing the reins to the boys.

'You will stay with us for a moon or two?' Striking Eagle asked.

The two boys watched for their answer, that they might know whether to unburden the horses and turn them out with the other horses.

Fallon hesitated, pressed with the urgency of his business, but unwilling to offend their hosts. The chief easily read his hesitation.

'It is not alone to visit as friends and family that you have come,' he stated, rather than asked.

Fallon hesitated a proper time to show his sorrow at such a breach of manners. He well knew how important it was to sit quietly, to visit of weather and game and omens the medicine man had seen, perhaps to smoke a pipe or two, shared around a circle, before any matters of importance were brought up. Ideally, any business would not be expected to be addressed before the third or fourth day.

He also knew the urgency of his mission. Even at the risk of being offensive, he had little time for formalities.

'There is a matter of much urgency to the Shoshone, and to me, that is in need of discussion by wise men and warriors.'

Striking Eagle studied his face a long moment, then nodded.

'Then your woman can go do what women do, when

they get together. We will come into my tepee and we will talk.'

Happily dismissed, and more excited than it would have been wise or prudent to show, Bird Shadow walked toward a tepee whose flap was held open in welcome. She could see several members of her family, as well as old friends waiting inside. She was no sooner inside than the tent flap was hastily dropped. It was an almost comical formality, to drop the flap. All sides of all the tepees were rolled up about two feet, for air to circulate away the summer's excessive heat. Immediately sounds common to womenfolk the world over emanated from the lodge, as if every woman there was talking, laughing, giggling, and squealing in delight, all at the same time. Fallon realized for the first time how deeply Bird Shadow must miss the relaxed friendships and relationships of her people. Somewhere in the back of his mind he vowed to bring her home to visit more often.

Because of the openness of all the lodges, Striking Eagle led the way to a tepee the most distant from the noise of the women. There, at the far edge of the village, they could talk unheard.

Silently they all followed Striking Eagle into the tepee and sat down cross-legged on furs and blankets. Fallon inconspicuously sat on a patch of bare ground, hoping to attract fewer of the crawling predators that he knew lurked within any form of fabric.

Several of the village's men had followed. They filed in and sat, until a solid circle of them lined the perimeter of the tent. They sat in silence for fully ten minutes until Striking Eagle spoke.

'It is well with Red Beard and his wife?'

'It is well,' Fallon replied.

'Is she yet with child?'

'The spirits have not yet blessed her stomach with fruitfulness.'

'Dark Hand, the mother of Bird Shadow, has asked Four Dogs, our medicine-man, for a portent. She grieves to have no grandchild.'

Fallon's eyes narrowed slightly.

'Has Four Dogs seen things in the world of spirits?'

The chief nodded. 'He says it was not a clear vision. He is not sure of its meaning. But he thinks that he understands. He thinks it is because you will not share your wife with those who are your friends, that the spirits have closed up her womb. The spirits are not happy when customs of friendship are not followed.'

Fallon worked to keep his face as inscrutable as theirs.

'It is good to have a word from one who sees into the world of the spirits. Perhaps it is because I am not of the Shoshone race, and because the customs of my people are very different from the customs of the Shoshone, that his vision was not as clear as Dark Hand must have hoped for. I will consider carefully his words. I must also weigh them against the sayings of the medicine-men of my own people. It is not easy for the two worlds to wed together.'

Silence followed his words for several minutes. No face showed expression except that of Hides From Bear. His emotion was too intense for even him to conceal. He said nothing, however.

At last Striking Eagle nodded once. Relief surged through Fallon, so great it was, once again, difficult to conceal.

134

The chief granted his permission for Fallon to tell them the purpose of his visit.

'What is the business that is so urgent to the white member of our village?'

Keeping any trace of urgency from his voice, Fallon said:

'Is the white man's ranch whose cattle bear the mark of a J, with a roof over it, known to all in the village?'

As he asked he reached out and brushed a spot of ground clear and smooth. Then he drew the Rafter J brand in the dirt, as it appeared on the Fanchers' cattle. Knowing grunts, some of them almost growls, emanated from every throat. The emotion betrayed by those sounds was clear as well in Striking Eagle's voice.

'It is known.'

'It is a sad thing to know that some of the white race do not appreciate the efforts of the Shoshone to live in peace with their white brothers.'

Grunts of agreement punctuated the thought.

'The name of the men who own that ranch is Fancher. There are two. They are brothers, without wives or children. It is said that if it were not for the white settlers of Long Valley they would make war against the Shoshone. Their hearts are greedy. They wish to have all the land, that nobody else may live on it.'

'But they let the white people in Long Valley live on it,' Striking Eagle disagreed.

'That is the new thing that I have come to share with my friends, with my wife's people. They have made a plan to make war on all those settlers, to kill them all. They will blame the Shoshone when they kill the white

135

settlers. Then they will send for the army to make war on all Shoshone peoples. They wish to have all the land for themselves.'

Uneasiness crept around the tepee, giving way quickly to a sense of outrage and anger.

'This is known by Red Beard to be true?'

'Many of the white people have heard them say such things.'

There was a long time of utter silence, which Fallon did not interrupt. Eventually Striking Eagle said:

'You have come with a plan that we should consider to deal with this danger to our people and our hunting ground?'

Fallon nodded. 'I have come to offer the hand of the white settlers to join together with the Shoshone against this threat. The Fancher brothers have hired many men as soldiers to fight this battle. It is not the place of the Shoshone to stand against them and their guns. I have come to seek an action by some of your young men that will sharpen their warrior skills without having to fight a war. An action that will give them opportunity to earn eagle feathers, without causing the army to send soldiers. An action that will let them become warriors in the manner of the great fighters of the Shoshone people. An action that will challenge the ability of the finest of your young men. An action that would stir the heart and thrill the soul of even the great Washakie.'

Interest clearly sparked, every man in the tent leaned forward to hear the plan of this red-bearded white man.

CHAPTER 17

It was two hours before dark when he rode in. He went straight to the ranch house, where he was met by Gus Fancher. Then he unsaddled his horse, fed and watered him, turned him into the corral without speaking to anyone. He came into the cookhouse when the bell rang, took a seat, and ate his supper in complete silence.

His eyes were hard as flint, unblinking, expressionless. They flitted about constantly, watching every corner, skimming across each face, never making eye contact with anyone. His mouth, except when it opened to accept a bite of food, was thin and hard.

At his hip was a well-polished gun butt, worn low, tied down. That he was a hired gunman nobody doubted for an instant. Several of his kind sat at the table, but even they made no offer to speak to him. Some of them even stole furtive glances edged in fear at the newcomer.

When he finished eating, he rose from the table and glided soundlessly from the room. After he left, conversation began to ripple here and there around the table. Someone at the table softly said: 'Orin Gregory.'

Total silence descended instantly, as if that name

snuffed out the courage of even hardened gunfighters. There was none of the usual easy banter in the bunkhouse that night, as tired hands fell into bed. Montana Smith watched from his own bunk, fighting the tight knot in his stomach.

He had come to work on the Rafter J after helping bring Fallon's herd to Long Valley. He, Russ Weathers and Joe Smith had all wanted to stay on and work for Fallon. Unfortunately, Fallon only had need for two hands. Montana had taken the initiative and opted to find another job. He hired on almost immediately with the Rafter J.

At first it had seemed a normal working ranch. Little by little over the past three months it had changed completely. There was more and more talk against squatters and sodbusters. There was more vitriol expressed about the Indians in the area. Then the ranch started hiring new hands, who worked no cattle and had no duties. They cleaned their guns. They target practiced. They competed against each other on occasion. They rode to town and caroused at One Eyed Jack's and the Pleasure Emporium. And they waited.

The waiting had become almost intolerable. Now the most notorious name any of them had ever heard had, apparently, joined the crew. There was no discussion of the matter. They all knew what it meant, what must come now. The feuds and squabbles the Fancher brothers had been having with the settlers in Long Valley had become steadily more open, more violent, more foreboding.

That sense of foreboding weighed on Montana with

increasing pressure. He knew he had to leave. Yet something kept him there. Some force he could not identify had seemed to whisper: 'Not yet,' in his ear, every time he determined to saddle up and ride out. Now the knot in his stomach told him the time had come.

'First light,' he promised himself, 'I'm outa here.'

One by one they drifted off to sleep. Some slept deeply. Some snored and mumbled. Some scratched or stretched or squirmed in their sleep. The moon settled beyond the horizon. Deep darkness spread across the land. Night animals scurried, their slight noises no longer heard. Horses in the corral stamped at flies or rubbed against a rail. Somewhere far off a lonely coyote's lament was almost inaudible.

Sometime in the middle of that deep darkness, rails lifted stealthily from the corral gate. A horse was led in total silence past dogs that lay in odd positions, sleeping. Or dead. In the middle of the yard, half-way between ranch house and bunkhouse, the horse squealed in sudden pain and fear. One small squeal, muffled, hardly heard, not even as loud as the thud of the horse's body against the ground.

Silently the door of the bunkhouse crept open. One cowboy, touched by some slight breath of air, stirred and turned over. His stirring was lost in the snores and mutterings of a sleeping crew.

Slowly the earth turned toward morning. Light crept furtively across the sleeping land. Night creatures scurried out of the open, into their daylight lairs.

That light filtered silently into the bunkhouse. Dreams began to fragment and melt away. Aching muscles and sore bones began once again to make their presence known. Full bladders began to send messages to stir and move.

One pair of eyes fluttered open, then closed, then open again. The body behind the eyes rolled over and sat up on the edge of the bunk. The eyes were drawn to a strange, dark blot in the center of the floor. He frowned. Something dripped into the blot. His eyes lifted upward, then jerked unnaturally wide.

'Yeaaaow! What in the Sam Hill?!' at the top of his lungs.

Pandemonium erupted. Every hand leaped to his feet, several with guns already drawn. Yells of query and surprise reverberated from the rafters. Then silence dropped a curtain across the room as total as if hearing suddenly ceased to exist. All eyes froze on the same horrifying image.

In the center of the room, hanging from a ceiling joist, a severed horse's head dripped blood into a puddle on the floor.

The first words any of them had heard the man called Orin Gregory speak broke the silence. A tight voice, dripping fury, let loose a string of epithets the like of which most of them had never heard, even in that rough, crude land.

Gregory dropped his gun into its holster, then whipped the holster around his fully dressed body. He swiftly tied it down, then lifted and dropped the gun back into the holster twice. He jerked on his boots, grabbed his hat, and rushed out the door.

The rest of the crew herded out behind him. Some were dressed. Some were in long underwear. Some weren't. All were barefoot or stocking-footed. They hurried in mincing steps on tender soles to follow the fabled gunman.

When he suddenly froze, they froze behind him like twenty lock-stepped shadows. Together they stared at the gunman's horse, minus the head, lying in the middle of the yard. Two dogs, looking sickly, sniffed the carcass. The other two still lay where they had been drugged or poisoned.

Gregory issued another string of epithets. He stalked to the ranch house. He pounded on the door. It opened almost instantly. Angry words were answered by puzzled, then defensive, then consoling tones.

The two Fancher brothers stepped off the porch and stared at the equine carcass. Every hand could hear Gregory. His voice was still low, charged with either fear or fury.

'You didn't tell me Injuns er haints was involved here! If them was Injuns did this, they wasn't no natural ones. I sleep light enough to hear a feather drop. I didn't sign up to fight no haints. And I sure didn't sign up to lose the best horse I ever owned. I'm gettin' my stuff. I'm ridin' outa here. When I come back with my stuff, you better have my saddle on the best horse you got, an' a bill o' sale fer that horse, er I'll hang both your heads right up there alongside that horse's.'

He strode toward the bunkhouse. The two Fanchers looked at each other. The anger in their eyes began to grow as their jaws set. One of them spoke.

'Whitey, put Gregory's saddle on Buck.'

Whitey rushed to comply with his orders, leading the rancher's finest personal horse, saddled, into the yard seconds before Gregory strode from the bunkhouse,

141

bedroll in hand. He rode out as silently as he had come.

Before he was out of the yard, three other gunmen knocked at the door of the ranch house, demanding their time. The trio rode out together within the hour.

They were scarcely out of sight when Slim Fancher ordered the cook to ring the dinner bell, assembling the crew. He rang it with the greater urgency one might have expected in such a time.

When the crew had all assembled, Gus Fancher came out and spoke.

'I've run outa patience. You boys get your stuff ready. Bring every gun you own. If you're short on ammunition, we've got plenty here. I don't want nobody runnin' out afore this night's over. By sundown we're gonna be at the broad end o' that valley. We'll go around through Russell's Canyon, so nobody from town will see us and hightail it up the valley with a warnin'. By daylight we're gonna be watchin' that squaw man's house burnin' behind his dead body. I want every house, every corral, every barn, every shed – even every outhouse – all the way up that valley, burnt to the ground. I want every sodbuster in the valley dead. You can do whatever you want with the women, but when you're done with 'em, I want them dead too. We're cleanin' out that nest o' varmits once an' fer all! Then we got enough Injun stuff ta string around to blame it all on the Shoshoni. This here's the day we take this country back.'

He stormed back into the ranch house, slamming the door behind him.

The remaining crew members looked at each other. Half a dozen smiled, an unnatural light in their eyes.

The rest looked either determined, resigned, or apprehensive.

Nobody noticed, just over an hour later, as Montana Smith led his horse quietly back into the trees behind the barn. Moving silently, keeping the trees between himself and the yard, he led him for 300 yards before he stepped into the saddle. Then he rode slowly, carefully, until he was a mile from the ranch yard. Then he spurred his mount to a long, purposeful lope.

CHAPTER 18

Tension stretched the atmosphere until the air itself seemed to hum. Buckboards and wagons, all turned on their sides, made a wide half-circle from edge to edge of the valley. The valley was wide. The settlers were few. The space between each bit of fortification was nearly a rifle shot.

It was deemed close enough. That meant anyone passing through any of those gaps would be within easy range of those behind the wagons.

If they hit their target. That was anything but a sure thing, Fallon fidgeted. These were settlers, farmers with families, not warriors. He and Ralph were the only ones among them that could stand against the hired gunmen of the Fanchers.

Then there was the possibility they would circle around, attack the center of the valley, and sweep both ways. In that event, there would be nobody even to slow the devastation they wreaked until they had already destroyed every home in the valley but this last one, at the valley's lower end. This one, too, would be destroyed then. They had no hope of repelling an attack from all sides, or even from two sides.

Against a determined foe, their defense from even one side was questionable.

Fallon walked the defense perimeter one more time, assuring himself it was as good as they were capable of making it. He mounted his horse and rode to the three sentries posted, making sure they were awake, alert, and aware of the importance of their post. He was there, well away from the homestead, when the last of the valley's settlers arrived at the Richmans. Their little farm looked almost like an Indian village, with tents ranged around for each family's campsite. The common area held a large fire, fueled constantly, at which one family or another was almost always either preparing or eating a meal.

Most of the day Bird Shadow and Martha Cranston had stood together, saying little. Some of the settlers kept a careful distance from them, darting furtive glances their way. A couple made remarks about 'that squaw' just loud enough to be 'accidentally' overheard. The two women appeared to neither hear nor notice.

Others, the majority in fact, made it a point to greet them, to stop by to chat, or to invite them to join one or another of the families. They demurred, spoke little, and were clearly preoccupied.

Late that morning the object of their concern appeared on the scene. Last of the settlers to arrive in response to the urgent summons carried the length of the valley, Big Jim and Wilma Turner wheeled their buckboard into the yard.

Jim jumped down from the seat and held up a hand for his wife. Instead of walking around to her side of the conveyance, he stayed where he had gotten down, forcing her to slide across the seat to take his hand and dismount. They turned and started toward the house, then stopped abruptly.

Unseen by them until that moment, Bird Shadow and Martha blocked their path. Confusion crossed Big Jim's face. He looked at Martha, then at Bird Shadow, then visibly dismissed them with a 'Mornin', ladies.'

Taking Wilma's arm he started to walk around them. Bird Shadow and Martha, moving as one, stepped sideways to block their path. Wilma looked startled, then frightened. She tried to step away from Jim, but his grip on her arm tightened. She winced slightly.

He frowned at the women.

'You ladies want somethin'?' he asked.

Martha smiled tightly.

'You don't recognize me, do you?'

The mini drama began to attract attention. Several of the settlers edged closer, listening intently to hear what was being said.

Jim's glance shot around the yard and came back to Martha, clearly confused.

'I don't know that I do. I seen the squaw here, in town. I don't recollect meetin' you.'

'Think back a ways, Jim. Maybe it wasn't as important to you as it was to me, but you ought to remember. You especially ought to remember the times you came into my bed when my mother was gone, and raped me.'

Audible gasps shot around the gathering group. People crowded closer to listen.

Jim's face paled. His jaw set. His grip on Wilma's arm tightened. She grimaced to keep from crying out.

'I don't know what you're talkin' about,' Jim insisted.

'Who are you?'

'I've changed, haven't I, Jim,' Martha said. Her voice was flat, not without emotion, but the words slapped with a flat feel, like a beaver's tail when it strikes the water. 'I'm not a frightened, helpless little girl any more.'

'I don't know what you're talking about,' he insisted.

'I'm Martha Forestal.'

Blood drained from Jim's face. He shot a glance around the still assembling crowd of settlers. 'Martha?' he breathed.

'The same,' Martha replied, spitting the words at him, as if they themselves would cut him in two. 'Little Martha Forestal, your step-daughter, whom you raped and abused until I ran away from home to get away from you. I've sent some telegrams, Jim. I found out how you and mother took in another young girl. A girl named Wilma Hodginson. Then my mother just disappeared, and you left the country. What happened, Jim? Did mother catch you raping another helpless girl, so you had to kill her and run away?'

'You're crazy!' Jim insisted. Sweat stood out on his forehead.

Martha continued: 'Wilma isn't your wife, is she, Jim? She's your slave. Just like you wanted me to be your slave.'

'You're crazy as a pet coon!' Jim yelled. 'She's my wife. Now get outa my way an' stop spreadin' a pack o' lies about me.'

'Did you murder my mother, Jim?'

When he didn't answer, she turned to Wilma. 'Is that what happened, Wilma? Did Jim kill my mother?'

147

Unexpectedly Wilma wrenched her arm out of Jim's grip. She stepped three steps away, clutching the fabric of the top front of her dress, gripping it with white knuckles. Her too-wide eyes stared wildly at Jim. But when at last she spoke her words were barely audible.

'He told me she'd been killed by a bear.'

'Did she catch you two together?' Martha pressed.

Wilma nodded. 'I couldn't stop him. He wouldn't never let me say no. After we got caught, he said we were going to go live somewhere else.'

As she talked, her voice began to gain strength. A tide of fear and shame and anger within her began to swell and flow, bursting the chains that had kept it so long in check. 'He told me I was goin' to be his wife, now, an' if I ever didn't do 'zactly like 'e tol' me to do, he'd kill me. An' when I up an' got pregnant, he beat me, an' then he made me get rid of it.'

What sounded almost like a sob was choked off before it quite made it from her throat. She began to shake, with fury, finally, instead of fear. She pointed a trembling hand at Jim. Her voice lifted to a wail.

'You made me kill my baby!'

'Shut up!' Jim spit at her. 'Shut your fool mouth an' get back in the wagon. We're leavin'.'

Martha's voice cut in hard and sharp.

'No you're not, Jim. You're not going anywhere. Wilma doesn't have to do anything you say any more. Neither do I. I'm not a little girl any more, Jim. I'm an old, hard, used woman, and I'll die before I let you walk away from here to ruin any more lives.'

As she spoke, a gun appeared from somewhere in the folds of her dress. It pointed unwaveringly at the center of Jim's chest.

Jim stared at the gun in her hand. He blinked several times. He looked at Wilma, then back at Martha. His glance danced around the circle of settlers again, shocked by the hard glares that met his gaze. He shook his head.

'You're crazy,' he said again. His voice almost shook. 'You're crazy. The whole lot of you, if you believe a word o' that. It's all lies. All lies. Wilma, get in the wagon.'

'Go to hell!' Wilma screamed back at him, backing another step.

The pallor in Jim's face fled before a red tide of anger. He glared at Martha. He gritted.

'You ain't got the guts to pull that trigger. You're just a two-bit whore that ain't worth a pimple on a hog's rear end. If you keep pointin' that gun at me, I'm gonna kill you in ten seconds, an' then I'm ridin' outa here.'

'If you think I won't kill you, just go for your gun,' Martha challenged.

He either thought she wouldn't, or thought she'd hesitate. She had never shot a man before. She did hesitate. That hesitation might have cost Martha her life.

He grabbed for his gun as he spewed a string of maledictions. Its barrel was clearing leather as a merest hint of indecision crossed Martha's face. Then a knife handle suddenly appeared jutting from the front of Jim's throat. The upward motion of his gun barrel stopped.

As the motion of his draw halted, Martha's second of indecision passed. She squeezed the trigger. Her gun roared and bucked. A hole appeared in Jim's shirt pocket. He staggered a step backward. The gun slipped

149

from his hand. He opened his mouth, as if to speak. A great stream of blood spewed outward. He sat down abruptly. He fell backward. His eyes and mouth gaped open. Blood welled up in his mouth and began to run from one corner of his lips. The flow stopped, and everything became motionless. The blood that filled his mouth, as if it were some macabre bowl, began almost instantly to darken on top.

Silence gripped the yard. Bird Shadow stepped forward and pulled her knife from Jim's throat. It made a small gurgling sound. She carefully wiped the blood from it, using the dead man's shirt. She returned it to its sheath and stepped back beside her friend. Martha still gripped her gun, still pointed at the spot Jim had stood.

Suddenly a well of tears sprang from her eyes, coursing down her cheeks. The gun sagged downward until it hung loosely at the end of her arm, then it dropped into the dirt. Several women rushed forward, putting their arms around Martha, leading her away, consoling, offering the strength of community. Only Bird Shadow was surprised that the tide of concern flowed around her as well, and she felt for the first time the hugs and pats and held hands of acceptance.

Wilma stood, forgotten and alone, as the group of women began to move away. Nobody noticed as she walked stiffly to the body on the ground. Nobody saw her bend over and lift the gun he had dropped as he died. Until it began firing, nobody even thought about her. At the first shot, everybody whirled, then watched in shock as Wilma fired a second, then a third, then a fourth, then a fifth bullet into the dead body.

Every person in the yard seemed sculpted in stone for several seconds. Then Bird Shadow separated herself from the grouped women and walked quickly to Wilma. Watching Wilma's face, already beginning to twist and distort with an impossible conflict of feelings, she gently took the gun from her limp hand. She tossed it aside on the ground. Acting in direct defiance of her well-ingrained customs, she put her arms around the young girl and pulled her to herself.

At once, Wilma began trembling violently. She collapsed against Bird Shadow as if all her bones had suddenly melted within her. Great sobs began to rack her slender body. Bird Shadow murmured softly into her ear. Afterward she could not have told what she said, nor did it matter. It was all of new beginnings and walking away from old wounds. It was about sunrises to come, whose beauty would slowly wipe away the terrors of nightmares past. It was about a promise to be, for her, someone she could talk to at last, someone to confide in, trust, who would care about her as a person.

The circle of support that had sprung up unexpectedly around Bird Shadow and Martha moved, as Bird Shadow built a picture of a world that could yet be, for Wilma. As it moved, encasing the trio in its embrace, it illuminated the first rays of hope Wilma had experienced in many months.

CHAPTER 19

'Rider comin' fast,' Ralph announced.

The words were unnecessary. Fallon had not only spotted the rider, he recognized him.

'It's Montana,' he said.

'The one who worked for you?'

Fallon nodded as they watched the other's approach. Ralph was the third of the sentries he had visited as he made the rounds. He had stayed to visit a short while. Now they waited together.

When Montana was well within hailing distance Fallon stepped out of the clump of trees and brush from which they watched.

Montana and his horse both started visibly before he recognized Fallon. He reined his horse toward his former boss and approached at a fast trot.

'You 'bout scared the liver outa me, Fallon. You boys the sentries, by chance?'

Instead of answering, Fallon said:

'Howdy, Montana. What brings you over this way? I thought you'd hired on with the Rafter J.'

Montana nodded. 'Yeah, I did. I'm headin' out.'

'You drew your time?'

152

'Nope. I just sorta slid out the back way. I got no stomach fer what the Fanchers got goin'.'

'That right?'

'I 'spect you know a whole lot more'n I kin tell ya,' Montana observed, 'but I rode over to tell ya what I know. Fanchers is comin' after you folks. They're maddern' a couple hornets what got a cow-pie stuck in their hive.'

Fallon resisted the urge to smile.

'Somethin' happen?'

Montana grinned suddenly.

'Well, ya might say that. They been bringin' in gun hands till I done got plumb uncomfortable. It's been clear fer a while they're fixin' to start a range war. Then this real bad fella rode in, that even the other gunfighters was a-scared of. Orin Gregory, his name is.'

Fallon's jaw clamped.

'I've heard of him.'

'Yeah, well he ain't there no more. It seems the mornin' after he got there, we all woke up an' his horse's head is hangin' from the ceilin' in the bunkhouse, drippin' blood. The rest o' the horse is lyin' out in the middle o' the yard. Not even the dogs heard nothin' er made a sound. Now you gonna tell me you don't know nothin' 'bout that there?'

Fallon smiled slightly.

'What happened then?'

'Gregory cussed out the Fanchers, started talkin' 'bout haints, whatever they are. . . .'

'Ghosts,' Fallon explained.

'Figgered as much. Anyway, he made Fancher give 'im another horse, an' he rode out. Three er four o' the

153

gunfighters followed 'im down the road. Fanchers is hoppin' mad. They tol' everybody to get loaded up an' grab as much ammunition as they kin carry. They're a-comin' to wipe out everythin' in the valley. Fanchers' orders is to burn every building, clear down to the outhouses, and kill every man woman an' child in the valley. Oh, he said they could use the women all they want first, but be sure they're dead when they get done. He's got it figgered to blame the Injuns. I waited fer a chance and slipped out through the timber. I don't want no part o' that deal. You treated me right. The folks in the valley is good folks. I wanted ya to know they're comin'.'

'You throwin' in with us?'

He shook his head.

'Naw, I can't quite do that. I've always rode fer the brand. It's took a bunch fer me to turn my back on that. Even knowin' what they are, I can't quite just turn around and start shootin' at the outfit I been workin' with. Some o' them boys ain't all bad. Naw, I'll jist ride out. At least I thought I could even the playin' field a mite afore I do.'

'Much obliged,' Fallon said. 'Did they say how they're comin'?'

'Well, yeah. As a matter o' fact they did. They're gonna circle around the town and ride through Russell's Canyon, so nobody close to town will spot 'em Then they're gonna start at Richman's place, an' wipe out everything all the way up to your place. They figger to hit Richman's just about dark.'

'Much obliged,' Fallon said again. 'That'll help. You ride careful.'

Montana nodded once. He wheeled his horse and rode off at a right angle to the road, putting distance between himself and an impossible conflict.

Fallon and Ralph watched him ride away in silence for a long while. When he was nearly a quarter-mile away, Ralph said:

'You thinkin' what I'm thinkin'?'

'Russell's Canyon?'

'It'd sure beat sittin' an' waitin' fer 'em on their terms. I always liked surprises.' Fallon nodded. 'You get the other sentries. I'll ride back to Richman's and get the bunch. We'll meet you at this end o' the canyon.'

Ralph nodded and walked to his horse. Fallon was nearly out of sight by the time he was in the saddle.

The arrogance of the rich and powerful sometimes borders on stupidity. It had never occurred to the Fanchers, nor, apparently, to any of their crew, that hunters may, at any time, become the hunted. They rode at a trot. Only the gunfighters maintained their habitual surveillance of their surroundings. Even they were relaxed. Some smiled in anticipation of the night's carnage and raping. Those who were normally just working cowboys rode stiffly, betraying their discomfort with what others anticipated with glee. Some talked as they rode, making no effort to keep their voices down. Bit rings jingled. Saddles creaked. Men coughed and cleared their throats. All in all, they made enough noise for those waiting in the rocks and brush to hear them fully half a mile before they appeared.

Russell's Canyon was hardly more than ten foot deep at any point. It was little more than a wide gully, dug by some ancient torrent of water that carried away everything softer than the surrounding soil and rock. It had left, along its edges, a few jagged boulders and countless seams and crevices. In most of those seams brush had sprung up, but the bottom of the canyon remained bare and flat. Its gravelly surface too inhospitable for vegetation, it provided a convenient road. The banks provided the concealment. It offered a way to ride past Boxelder without the danger of anyone there being aware of their passing.

From the end of the canyon it would be another hour's ride until they reached the Richman homestead. From then until daylight they would vent the Fanchers' wrath on the squatters who dared to create a problem for the mighty cattle barons who first settled that area. They had wrested their ranch from the forces of nature, from the threat of Indians, from wild animals, and from outlaws and rustlers. They would once and for all rid it, now, of this latest threat to their sole use of its resources.

'That's far enough!' A hidden voice barked like a rifle shot.

Every pair of eyes in the group began to cast wildly about for the source of the command. Gus Fancher bristled.

'Who's there? Show yourself!'

Fallon stepped out into the flat gravel of the canyon's bed, a hundred feet in front of the Fancher brothers where they rode at the van of their would-be army. At waist-level he held the Colt revolving shotgun he had last used against the Arikara. It was pointed at the leading one of the two ranchers.

'Gus, Slim,' Fallon addressed the pair, 'it's all over.

You ain't ridin' roughshod over this country any more.'

He raised his voice, knowing the sides of the canyon would carry it easily to every man in the group. 'You boys are outgunned and outflanked. You can throw down your guns now and ride away, or you can die like fish in a barrel. It's your choice.'

Hidden homesteaders let glimpses of their hats or their gun barrels show for brief instances, to lend credence to Fallon's threat. There was fully half a minute of dead silence. A cowboy close to the back of the pack spoke up.

'I'm outa here.'

He reined his horse out of the bunch and started to retreat the way he had come. Slim Fancher turned in the saddle.

'Nobody runs out on me!' he yelled.

His pistol leaped into his hand and barked, sending a bullet squarely between the shoulders of the retreating cowboy, who threw up his arms and pitched wordlessly from the saddle.

Slim whipped his gun back to Fallon, but before he could aim he was thrust backward out of the saddle by a blast of buckshot from Fallon's shotgun. He hadn't hit the ground yet when it roared again, and his brother followed him into a dark oblivion. All along the canyon, bedlam erupted.

Some sat in the saddle, firing at anything that moved. Others dived to the ground, seeking cover behind anything they could find.

Fallon had stationed the settlers too perfectly, too carefully. They had a clear field of fire that covered every spot in the narrow canyon. It was over in minutes.

The Fancher brothers were the first to fall, within the space of a single second, to the fury of Fallon's weapon. The gunfighters, who posed the greatest threat, were swiftly dispatched as well. With no place to run or hide, and no chance to use their hard-earned skills with their weapons, they were as helpless as any other man. They fired wildly at anything they could see. They died within seconds of one another, their bodies riddled by a hail of bullets. Three Rafter J hands had instantly thrown their hands high in the air and sat their horses. They sat, unscathed, as the brief battle rattled down to silence.

A horse, squealing in pain, thrashed about on the ground. Fallon stepped forward, walking to the wounded animal. Holding his pistol at the top and back of the suffering animal's head, he fired once. The horse fell silent. He turned his attention to the three surviving hands.

'Did Fancher send anyone any other way?'

The closest cowboy to him shook his head, careful to keep his arms high.

'It never occurred to either one of 'em you folks might fight back. They was jist plumb determined to kill everyone in the valley.'

'You're riding with them.'

He nodded, helpless to keep his face from losing its color.

'I can't argue with that. But we didn't have no stomach for it. If we'da tried to leave, one o' the Fanchers, or one o' their gunmen, woulda jist killed us, like Slim did Keith. We figured maybe when things started we'd get a chance to ride off. I sure wasn't gonna kill no women er kids, I kin tell ya that.'

By the time he fell silent, the settlers had all risen or stepped from their places of concealment. Fallon turned his attention to them.

'Anyone get hit?'

Considering the number of dead men lying on the canyon floor, it might have seemed the silliest of questions. Nobody noticed. Silence hung for a heartbeat, then Luther Grimes spoke.

'I got nicked a little. Lost half an ear.'

Fallon allowed himself a smile of satisfaction.

'Anyone got any objections to letting these three boys ride out?'

Nobody answered. He addressed the three.

'You boys can go back to the Rafter J and gather your stuff. You best ride out of the country.'

They wasted no time accepting the offer. The sound of their fleeing hoof-beats hadn't stopped echoing from the canyon walls when Fallon spoke again.

'Let's let our families know we're all right, then we'll have to bring some wagons back and bury the dead.'

Every man there was instantly filled with an overwhelming urgency to see his wife and family – to go home. Fallon's thoughts turned to a comment he hadn't had time until now to consider. What did Bird Shadow mean by that comment, just before he left? What was it she had said?

He strained to remember, then her words came back to him. *When you return, I will explain why these buckskins are growing so tight on my stomach.*

'Now what in the world could she have meant by that?' he mused as he rode.

159

Then realization swept through him. Nobody in the bunch understood why he suddenly let out a loud war whoop and spurred his horse to a dead run.